LOVE & MURDER

LORRAINE BARTLETT
L. L. BARTLETT

Polaris Press

DESCRIPTION

Abused: A Daughter's Story: *Emily Miller knew her life was about to change forever the day her mother said, "I'm pregnant." She'd hear those words again and again—and with every pregnancy Emily's father changed from bad to worse. For years the Miller family suffered through his rages. It took a terrible loss for the family to regroup, and all the love Emily can muster to save her siblings.*

Cold Case *. . . the short story that inspired the 4th Jeff Resnick book, BOUND BY SUGGESTION. Psychic Jeff Resnick has no expectations when investigating the disappearance of a four-year-old, until he confronts the mind responsible—a shattering experience for all involved.*

An Unconditional Love*: A one-night stand changes Leslie Turner's life forever when she discovers she's pregnant. Keeping the child means losing her business. Even more devastating, the baby is born with a disfiguring birth defect. Her carefully planned life falls apart . . . until years later when she once again meets her baby's father. Can they ever be a family?*

We're So Sorry, Uncle Albert: *The Nichols family is all in a tizzy when it's discovered their penny-pinching Uncle Albert is worth millions, and decide he has overstayed his worldly welcome. But can they bump off the old man and get away with it?*

Love Heals: *It's the most romantic night of the year and Diana Mason is alone. She broke up with her boyfriend because he wanted a play-mate not a soul mate, but it's someone else who haunts her thoughts on the most romantic of holidays. Is there a chance he's thinking of her, too?*

Prisoner of Love*: Rhonda Roberts went looking for love in all the wrong places, and found it through an ad in the personals section of her local newspaper. Family and friends think she's crazy when she becomes engaged to a convicted felon, and the lengths she'll go to see him set free.*

Blue Christmas: *Christmas used to be a joyous time for Judi Straub, but that was before her parents passed away and her siblings became too busy to socialize with their old maid sister. Holidays spent with friends were a nightmare. Then one late December Judi won an all-expense-paid trip to Puerto Rico where Harry Powell swept her off her feet. But her fantasy of happily-ever-after was quickly derailed. Would Judi always have a Blue Christmas?*

Also By Lorraine Bartlett

THE VICTORIA SQUARE MYSTERIES
A Crafty Killing
The Walled Flower
One Hot Murder
Dead, Bath and Beyond (with Laurie Cass)
Yule Be Dead (with Gayle Leeson)
Murder Ink (with Gayle Leeson)
Recipes To Die For: A Victoria Square Cookbook

LIFE ON VICTORIA SQUARE (*A companion series to the Victoria Square Mysteries*)
Carving Out A Path
A Basket Full of Bargains
The Broken Teacup
It's Tutu Much
The Reluctant Bride

THE LOTUS BAY MYSTERIES
Panty Raid (A Tori Cannon-Kathy Grant mini mystery)
With Baited Breath
Christmas At Swans Nest
A Reel Catch

BLYTHE COVE MANOR
A Dream Weekend
A Final Gift
An Unexpected Visitor
Grape Expectations

TALES OF TELENIA (adventure-fantasy)
THRESHOLD
JOURNEY
TREACHERY

SHORT STORIES
Love & Murder: A Collection of Short Stories
Happy Holidays? (A Collection of Christmas Stories)
An Unconditional Love
Love Heals
Blue Christmas
Prisoner of Love
We're So Sorry, Uncle Albert

Writing as L.L. Bartlett
THE JEFF RESNICK MYSTERIES
Murder On The Mind
Dead In Red
Room At The Inn
Cheated By Death

Bound By Suggestion
Dark Waters
Shattered Spirits

❋ Created with Vellum

Would it surprise you to learn that I got my start as a writer by selling short stories? I like to write about women with problems and how they cope. When adversity strikes, sometimes all we *can* do is cope. Sometimes, we do better.

The first market I tried was for sweet romances, and guess what—I'm still writing them because I enjoy them (and I hope you enjoy them, too). But I'm known for my New York Times bestselling mystery novels, and I've included two of my mystery shorts in this collection.

My thanks go to Judy Beatty and Martha Paley Francescato for their super proofing.

I hope you enjoy this sample of my writing.

Happy Reading!

Chapter One

ABUSED

A Daughter's Story

by L.L. Bartlett

"Take the picture," Daddy said from behind me.

"I don't want to."

"Take it," he grated, and I knew from bitter experience not to defy one of Daddy's orders.

I brought the little camera's viewfinder up to eye level and framed the shot. Mama looked almost pretty, dressed in a new floral print blouse, her hair neatly arranged and make-up blush staining her cheeks. I wanted to believe she was only asleep, that the past five years hadn't happened. But they had, and nothing could ever erase the events that had led to this day.

I squeezed off a shot, then another. I didn't want Daddy to say I hadn't done my best to obey him.

"Now get one of the whole coffin," he said. "I'm paying a lot of money for this funeral, and I want to be able to show it off for years to come."

Take it yourself, I wanted to scream. I thought it indecent of him to make me do this. What would the neighbors think? Besides, I wanted to remember Mama alive, her head thrown back, her vibrant laugh rattling the windows. But she hadn't been like that for years. She hadn't had anything to laugh about for a long, long time.

I stood back and took another two pictures, then handed him the camera.

"I don't feel well," I said. "I'm going to sit down for a while."

Daddy's face twisted into a scowl. "This is how life turns out, girl. We're all gonna end up dead. Even you—so get used to it."

I looked away. Meeting his gaze would only be seen as a challenge, and I wasn't about to do that here at the funeral parlor. Fighting tears, I slowly turned and headed for a row of chairs.

Our neighbors were clustered in knots, talking and occasionally laughing. My little sister, Amber, sat in one of the chairs, her hollow-eyed stare focused on the floor. She hadn't spoken much in the two days since Mama died, and I was worried about her.

"This wasn't supposed to happen," she murmured, turning her grief-stricken eyes toward me.

"What, honey?" I asked, glad to hear her young voice. She was almost eleven. I was seventeen.

"The doctor said she'd be home in a couple of weeks. He said she'd get better. I didn't just dream it. You heard him say so, too, didn't you, Emily?"

Amber's tear-filled blue eyes bore into mine, breaking my heart.

"Nobody's perfect," I said gently, and put my hand on her shoulder, brushing back her long blonde hair. "Even doctors can make mistakes."

"What's gonna happen to us now?" she asked, her voice cracking.

I had to swallow before I could answer. There was no way I could take away all her fears—I had too many myself.

"Now that Daddy's home, we'll just have to make the best of it."

"I don't want to live with *him*," she growled. She tried to look at the coffin, but couldn't seem to make herself do it. "*He* did this to her. He'll kill us, too."

"You'll be fine. I'll take care of you—and the others. You'll see."

"But it'll never be better. We'll always be unhappy with *him*."

For one so young, Amber had seen enough misery to last a lifetime. We all had.

I sat back in my chair and thought about the day Mama came home from the doctor's office with a big smile on her face, her eyes alight with glee. "I'm pregnant," she said and crouched down to kid level. "Do you know what that means, Emily?"

I was six years old at the time. "A new baby?" I guessed.

"That's right."

"We don't need a new baby," I told her.

"Oh yes we do," she said. "But don't worry; you'll always be Mama's big girl."

My brother Bobby was five back then. We lived in a small but comfortable house, and Bobby and I had our own bedrooms.

"Where's the baby going to sleep?" I asked suspiciously, feeling threatened that my life would have to change.

"If it's a girl, in your room," Mama said. "If it's a boy, he'll sleep with Bobby. But no matter what, I'm going to let you pick out new curtains and a new bedspread so everything will look pretty. Wouldn't you like that?"

I remember staring at my scuffed brown school shoes, not at all happy with the prospect of sharing my living space with some crying baby.

"I'd rather have a puppy. Couldn't we get a puppy instead?" I asked.

Mama just smiled and went back into the kitchen.

After a few months, I did get used to the idea of a new baby, and even started to look forward to the prospect. Then one morning it was Daddy who woke me up and told me to get ready for school, which had never happened before.

"Where's Mama?" I asked, getting out of bed, already started tucking in the blanket and sheet. Daddy had been in the Marines and wouldn't tolerate an unmade bed.

"I took her to the hospital last night. You've got a new baby sister."

My elation turned to apprehension. I had been planning on a brother. I'd been so sure it would be a boy I'd insisted that Mama put the crib in Bobby's room. Now I'd have to move my toy box and make room for all the other junk Mama had accumulated for this baby.

"Wash up and get dressed," Daddy told me.

Three days later, Mama brought the new baby home. Little Amber was bright red and looked like a doll. Mama let me hold her and told me I'd be in charge of powdering her butt at changing time. It seemed like an important job, and I took it seriously.

Sharing a room wasn't so bad. I just had to be quiet when the baby slept. Mama let me sprinkle baby powder on when she changed Amber's diaper, and let me feed her. It was like having a living doll. As Amber got older, I kept all my good toys on the closet's high shelf; otherwise, she would throw them around the room and break them.

There was a lot more laundry, and the house seemed smaller with all the baby items cluttering the living room and kitchen, but we all got used to it.

Amber was two when Mama got pregnant again.

"How the hell could you let that happen?" Daddy shouted.

The door to their bedroom was closed and Bobby and I exchanged worried glances. Daddy's temper was well known. A closed door meant trouble and even Amber seemed to understand that something bad was about to happen. She started to cry, and I quickly took her upstairs. I sat down on my bed, pulled her onto my lap and tried to distract her by singing, but every time she heard a crash downstairs, her cries would get louder.

"Don't cry, baby, don't cry," I soothed her, afraid Daddy might take his anger out on her, too.

I heard Bobby's running footsteps flying up the stairs and the door to his room slam. I didn't need to look inside to know that he'd thrown himself down on his bed, pillow clasped around his ears, to help muffle his own sobs. My heart was pounding. This was the worst fight my parents had ever had.

Eventually, the door slammed and everything went deadly quiet. I heard the roar of the engine on Daddy's car and the squeal of tires on the driveway. He'd come back late at night and things would be strained for a few days, but it would be okay, I kept telling myself.

I went downstairs to check on Mama. She stood over the dryer, wiping silent tears from her cheeks.

"Is everything okay?" I timidly asked.

She sniffed and nodded. "It will be, baby. Don't you worry about it."

I watched her fold our clothes, separating them into little piles, and waited patiently until she'd finished. "I'll put them away."

Her mouth trembled and she stifled a sob. "Thank you, Emily. You've been a big help."

I threw my arms around her and she bent down to kiss the top of my head. "I'll help you, Mama. Don't worry."

Mama had a black eye the next morning. When I asked her about it, she said she'd walked into a door. She tried to laugh it off and changed the subject—once again telling me what a big help I was to her.

"And I'm going to need even more of your help when the new baby comes," she said and ran hot water into the sink.

"Another one?" I asked with dread.

"It's a blessing," Mama said, but her voice cracked.

"Does this mean we aren't going to get a dishwasher? Daddy promised you a dishwasher."

"We'll make do without one. We always have," she said and slid the breakfast dishes into the suds. "Now get ready for school."

I prayed even harder than the last time. This time it *would* be a boy. Mama said Amber would get a bed to match mine, and the crib would go in Bobby's room.

But it wasn't a boy.

"Another girl?" I wailed when Daddy told us the news one Sunday morning.

"Her name is Dorothy. Named after Grandma." But Amber couldn't say Dorothy so we called her Dee-Dee.

"This new baby is going to be a lot of work. I expect you to help your mother out," Daddy said. "Do you know how to run the washing machine?"

"No."

"Well, it's time you learned."

I also learned to wash dishes, mop floors, mow the lawn, and I always seemed to be changing diapers. I couldn't go out to play after school because Mama always needed help with something.

"You're the oldest," she'd tell me when Bobby would slip away to play softball with his friends. "It's your responsibility to help." I couldn't say no to any plea for help that Mama made. She always looked so tired. Somehow, I managed to keep my resentment bottled up.

Sometimes my friend, Jeannie, would come over to keep me company. She thought it was fun to change diapers and fold laundry—and I let her think so. "It's like playing house," I told her, but for me, it wasn't child's play. She seemed to enjoy it, but as an only child, she didn't have to do it on a daily basis. And when she went home, she could watch TV and play with her kitten.

Even though Daddy worked two jobs, there never seemed to be enough money. The fridge was always stocked with food and beer, but there wasn't any money left for fun things like movies or new toys for us kids.

Daddy belonged to two bowling teams, and once in a while he'd take Bobby and me fishing on his big blue boat, but those trips had become scarce after Amber was born, and never happened at all after Dee-Dee arrived. He still kept the boat. It sat in our driveway during the fall and winter months. We didn't know where he took it in the summer, but he'd disappear early on his days off and reappear with a pail of fish. Bobby and I learned how to gut and skin them, wrap them in butcher paper, and put them in the freezer. Daddy never seemed to eat the fish, and I'd sometimes see Mama wrap them in newspaper and stuff them in the garbage cans on trash days.

Dee-Dee was only five months old when I heard Mama crying on the phone one day.

"He's gonna kill me," she kept saying over and over again, her eyes filled with panic. The last time I'd seen that kind of fear had been when she'd told Daddy she was pregnant with Dee-Dee.

But she couldn't be pregnant—not again. Not so soon.

My stomach felt tight, and I felt on the verge of tears for the rest of the day, worrying about what would happen when Daddy found out.

Mama put Dee-Dee to bed early and sent Bobby, Amber and me to the neighbors that evening before Daddy came home from his second job. I remember Mrs. Boyd looking worriedly out the window. When she saw Daddy storm out the door and get into his car, she told her husband to watch us and hurried over to our house.

Bobby and Amber were watching TV and didn't seem to notice, glad because they got to see some old sitcom instead of Daddy's stupid game shows, but I stayed glued to the window, terrified.

It seemed like hours before Mrs. Boyd came back and took us home. The kitchen was immaculate, and the laundry was neatly folded on the old scratched coffee table. Mama sat on our worn, old couch with an ice pack held to her cheek.

She never mentioned her pregnancy to us kids, but soon she was wearing maternity clothes again.

Christopher was born the day after Dee-Dee's first birthday. We thought it was neat that, in the future, the new baby and Dee-Dee could share their birthdays, and I was glad because this time a crib would definitely go in Bobby's room.

Daddy never seemed to be home, and when he was around, he was always screaming at us, issuing orders, and telling us we were stupid and a liability to him. Other fathers cut the grass, took their kids to softball games, and came to the school's open house, but Daddy never did. He was either working or off with his buddies.

My friend Jeannie came over less and less.

"You're no fun," she finally told me at school one day. "All you ever do is work around the house. You can never go to Girl Scouts or the movies. You're just boring!"

I came home crushed. She'd been the only real friend I had. There were tears in Mama's eyes when I told her, but Chris started to cry and I could smell his diaper. Dee-Dee had been sick all day and had just thrown up on her high chair.

"I'll take care of Chris," I said grudgingly, seeing Mama had her hands full, and dragged him into Mama's room.

I hated that new baby. All he ever did was cry and mess his clothes.

"It's all your fault," I told him, as I pulled the soiled diaper from around his narrow hips, throwing it into the diaper pail. "Ever since you came, life's been even crappier around here."

Little Chris screwed his face into a frown and began to cry.

"Shut up!" I hollered, but the baby only began to wail louder.

"I said SHUT UP!" And for good measure, I pinched him. "There, now you've got something to cry about."

"Emily!" Mama snapped from the doorway.

She picked up the howling baby, getting his poop all over her shirt. "Don't cry, baby," she crooned, then turned her angry gaze on me. "Where did you ever learn such cruelty?"

Without even thinking, I blurted, "From Daddy."

Her eyes widened in horror. "What do you mean?"

"He always does that to Amber or Dee-Dee when they cry. Once he pinched Bobby so hard he left a big bruise on his arm."

Mama sank down on the bed, tears streaming down her cheeks. She looked ugly, her thin, white face pinched, and for the first time I noticed her drab brown hair was streaked with gray. Three babies in four years had turned Mama into an old woman.

Soon, she was sobbing as hard as Chris.

My stomach churned in panic, and I threw my arms around her. "I'm sorry, Mama, I won't do it again. I promise. Please stop crying," and then I realized that I was crying, too. I could hear Dee-Dee in the kitchen and saw Amber standing in the doorway, tears streaming down her little red cheeks.

Daddy came home late that night. Always a light sleeper, I awoke when I heard raised voices coming from the living room. I closed the bedroom door, so as not to wake Amber and Dee-Dee, and tiptoed halfway down the stairs so I could hear better.

"To think that you would hurt one of your own children," Mama was saying.

"A little discipline never hurt anyone," Daddy countered.

"But to pinch a crying baby—"

"You're too damned soft on all those kids. Now come on, take off that nightgown and come to bed."

"No, I won't. We don't have any rubbers and you'll be the first to scream if I end up knocked up again. Besides, I'm tired of being at your beck and call. You could at least show me some affection when we make love, instead of—"

"I don't want to hear about it," Daddy cut her off, and I crept back upstairs. I pulled the covers up to my chin and shivered, even though it wasn't cold.

I was afraid. Again. And I felt a lot older than my eleven years.

After the pinching incident, Mama tried not to depend on me so much, but I could see that being a full-time mother of five kids—two of them in diapers—and keeping up with cooking and laundry was often more than she could handle. I helped out as much as I could and tried not to get angry that I'd been forced to take on more than any child should. And I avoided Daddy as much as possible.

As the months dragged on, it seemed like we saw less and less of Daddy. Mama always said he was working, but we never seemed to have any more money.

Christopher was about eighteen months old when I realized the extent of the trouble in my parents' marriage. I came home from school and found Mama crying while she folded clothes.

"What's wrong?" I asked.

She wiped her nose on a tissue and continued to fold Christopher's hand-me-down baby clothes. "Nothing. I've got something in my eye."

The phone rang and the baby started to cry. "Go check on Chris," Mama said, and I dutifully went upstairs to get him up from his nap.

When I came back down, I grabbed a diaper and started to change him. I could hear Mama on the phone, talking to Grandma and strained my ears to hear Mama's end of the conversation.

"Darlene Murray saw them at the bowling alley. She left at the same time they did and said they got into Rob's car. Then they drove off. She stopped at the grocery store and saw his car again, parked in that same apartment complex." She paused. "I don't know. Two months ago, he told me it was over. And you know I don't believe in divorce. It wouldn't be good for the children. Besides, I haven't even talked to him about it yet." She paused again. "I know. But I can't push him into anything. What would we do if he left? You know how vindictive he can be."

I finished changing Chris's diaper, slung him on my hip, and went into the living room.

When Mama saw me, her face froze, going white.

"I can't talk any more. I'll call you later. Yes, I promise. Bye." She hung up.

"It isn't nice to listen in on other people's telephone conversations," Mama said, using her most stern voice.

"It isn't nice for a man to cheat on his wife and family, either," I said.

Mama's mouth dropped open, her cheeks blushing dark pink.

"We don't need him, Mama. We can make out just fine without him."

"Don't even think such a thing," she said. "And don't you dare say anything to Bobby or anyone else about this."

"No, Mama," I said.

She took Chris from my arms. "Finish folding the wash, will you? I have to go make supper." She headed for the kitchen.

Probably macaroni and cheese—from a box—again. That's all we ever seemed to eat. I folded the laundry and put it away, my mind whirling with what I'd heard. So Daddy had a girlfriend. I wasn't surprised. But the thought of divorce didn't frighten me. I worried more about him hurting Mama or one of the kids during one of his drunken rages.

That night, after all us kids had gone to bed, I was awakened by shouting. Daddy was terribly angry, and Mama was screaming at him. I slipped out of bed and crept to the top of the stairs, but the fight seemed to be over.

"Get out!" she yelled.

"You're damn right I'll go, and I'm not coming back," he hollered. The door slammed, then it was quiet.

I tiptoed back into my bedroom and looked out of the window, watched Daddy march to his car. He got in but didn't start the engine. He sat there for what seemed like a long time. I could hear Mama crying downstairs, but I was afraid to go to her. Afraid of him.

What if he came back inside? What if he started hitting Mama?

At last, Daddy's car door opened and he stalked toward the house. The door must've been locked, so he began to kick it. I didn't know if Mama opened it or if he busted it down, but soon he was back inside and the yelling started again.

I turned and saw Amber curled up in a ball on her bed. "No, no," she kept murmuring.

Bobby's bedroom door burst open. His face was twisted with fury. "He'd better not hit her—I'll kill him if he tries to hit her," he cried and flew down the stairs.

"Bobby, no!" I hollered, but he wouldn't listen.

"Get out of here—we don't want you," Bobby yelled, charging at Daddy like a poodle on a linebacker.

Daddy was saying something, lunging for Mama as I rounded the bottom of the stairs, but Bobby jumped between them, his arms swinging.

"Bobby, no!" Mama cried.

Without thinking, I went to Daddy's gun case, pulled out a shotgun and aimed it at Daddy's chest.

It was loaded.

"Emily, put that gun down," Mama screamed.

"Bobby, get out of the way," I said. My voice sounded shaky.

"Emily, you damn fool, put that thing down," Daddy thundered, but he didn't step forward.

"Get out, or I'll shoot you," I said, as the heavy gun wobbled in my grasp. "Bobby, call the police."

Daddy's eyes grew wild with suppressed rage. "You've poisoned my own children against me," he growled at Mama.

"We don't like you because you're so mean and you hurt Mama," Bobby yelled.

"Go away and don't bother us anymore," I said, the gun still leveled at Daddy. When he didn't move, I took a step forward. For the first time in my life, I felt powerful. In control. I wasn't going to let my bully of a father win this time.

Daddy's face was beet red, but he backed toward the door. "This is all your fault, Janet," he said, glaring at Mama. "I'll get you for this."

"Get out," I said again.

The door slammed. Mama, Bobby and I stared at it until we heard the sound of Daddy's car engine rev. He left rubber in the driveway as he took off, then it was deadly quiet, except for the sound of a crying baby.

I let the shotgun's barrel droop. Mama stepped forward, taking it from me. In one smooth action, she unloaded it.

"Emily, don't you ever touch a gun again," she said.

"Then let's get rid of them," I said. "Let's get rid of all Daddy's stuff!"

Even though it was after midnight, Mama and I started packing Daddy's things in cartons and trash bags, while Bobby went upstairs and quieted the baby.

"No matter what happens, you can't take him back," I told Mama, sounding more like a parent than a child.

"I won't," she promised. "But I don't know how we'll make it without his money. We may not be able to keep the house. But I promise Emily, you children and I will always be together."

She broke down sobbing, and I put my arms around her,

comforting her like I wished she could comfort me. I had to be strong for her. And suddenly I realized I was no longer a child.

Daddy didn't come back the next day, but one of his buddies came to pick up some of his stuff. I don't know what Mama did with the guns, but they were gone, and the case was empty after that.

Daddy didn't send any money, so Mama found a job as a sales-clerk at the mall. She worked from four until ten most evenings, as she had to wait for me to come home from school to take care of the rest of the kids. She was dead tired every day, but she actually seemed younger—and definitely happier. And none of us kids missed Daddy—only his paycheck.

We had a garage sale and sold the rest of Daddy's stuff. Mama frowned as she counted the dollars and change. "It's enough to pay the mortgage for a month, but that's all."

One of our neighbors knew someone at legal aid, who got Daddy's pay garnished, which helped a lot. Bobby wanted to get a paper route, but Mama wouldn't let him.

"Get good grades at school. Then when you grow up, you can get a well-paying job to take care of your family. I know you'd never abandon your kids," she said, and her voice cracked.

Our lives settled into a quiet rut. We did eat macaroni and cheese most nights, but Bobby's and my grades at school also improved. We really thought things were going to work out.

Then Daddy started coming around.

At first, he didn't seem quite so mean. He'd bring groceries and drink coffee with Mama at the kitchen table.

When the lawn mower broke, Mama called him, and Daddy

came over and fixed it. But he still made Bobby cut the grass.

Daddy showed up on Amber's birthday, bringing her a beautiful porcelain doll. But when she spilled punch on the doll's dress, he yelled at her and made her cry. Nobody felt happy as we morbidly sang Happy Birthday. Amber blew out the candles on her cake, glaring at Daddy. She didn't need to tell me what she'd wished for.

One day I came home from school and found Daddy's car parked in the driveway. I knew he should have been at work—and I had a bad feeling in my stomach. He was sitting in his old chair with a bottle of beer in his hand, watching TV.

"What're you doing here?" I said, unable to keep the anger from my voice.

"I live here," he said, looking smug.

I glared at him, wishing I could wipe the arrogant look from his face. Instead, I rushed into the kitchen. "You let him come back?" I accused Mama, unable to keep the panic from my voice.

"You don't understand," she said and pulled me into a hug. "The store closed and I lost my job. I didn't know what else to do. Emily, we *need* him. And he promised me it would be better this time. He promised."

"And what if it isn't? What if he's just as mean as he always was? What if he hits you again?"

"It won't happen," Mama said, but her eyes looked worried.

Daddy had taken the day off from work to move back in, and the whole family was crowded around the kitchen table for supper that evening. To celebrate his return, Daddy bought steaks. But Dee-Dee didn't want to eat hers and pushed her plate away, spilling her milk all over the bowl of mashed potatoes. Daddy hollered, making Dee-Dee cry, and Amber went running from the table. She hid under her bed and Mama had no luck getting her to come out. Daddy started yelling, and then all the little ones were crying. Daddy stormed out of the house, and we all went to bed early—even Mama.

It was late when Daddy came home drunk. He picked a fight with Mama and hit her—just like old times. This time Bobby called the police. The patrol car showed up with lights flashing, and when the cops saw Mama's face, they hauled Daddy away. All the neighbors were peeking through their curtains to see the show, and Mama threw herself on her bed and cried herself to sleep.

The next morning, Daddy was released, but we didn't see him much for a few days as he had to go back to work. He blamed Bobby for having to spend a night in jail, and that weekend punished him. Bobby had to wash all the windows on the house, including those on the second story.

"Rob, he's too young! He'll fall off the ladder and hurt himself!" Mama cried.

"Aw, you worry too much."

Bobby was awful mad, but he knew better than to do a sloppy job. Daddy wouldn't even let him stop for lunch, and it was almost three o'clock when Bobby finished.

Daddy came outside to inspect the work. "Looks pretty good," he said. Then he took the bucket from Bobby's hand, dumped dirt in it, and threw dirty water on all of the downstairs windows.

"Now you can do the whole job over again."

Bobby just stood there until Daddy went back into the house, then he started to cry.

"I hate that bastard," Bobby growled.

"Don't let Daddy hear you talk like that or you'll feel his belt," I warned him.

"I'll call the cops if he hits me again."

"And then we'll all be in even more trouble, and you know he'll take it out on Mama."

Bobby kicked the sponge and it got dirty. He rinsed it, and started on the windows again.

I felt sorry for Bobby, but I wasn't allowed to help him, so I snuck him a couple of cookies to keep him going until supper.

The house was very quiet that night. Even Dee-Dee and Christopher had learned to keep out of Daddy's way.

No matter what Mama did, she could never seem to please Daddy. She wanted to keep on working, but Daddy told her, "No wife of mine is going to work."

That lasted a couple of weeks.

"Starting tomorrow, I've got a job at a convenience store," Mama told me one day. "It's just weekday evenings. You'll have to watch the kids, but this way we'll have some money if Daddy should move out again."

I knew then that she wasn't thinking if he moved out —but when.

Only two weeks passed before Daddy found out about Mama's job. They had another big fight late that night, and once again I crept to the top of the stairs to listen.

"I told you, I don't want my wife working."

"Is that what you tell your girlfriend?" Mama accused.

I heard the crack of an open palm on another's skin.

"You leave Cheryl out of this," Daddy said.

I sank down on the stair, shaking with anger. How could any woman in her right mind want a man like Daddy? Why had Mama put up with him for so long?

I snuck back to bed and it was my turn to cry myself to sleep.

When I came home from school the next day, Mama was folding the last of Daddy's shirts, putting them into a cardboard carton while silent tears streamed down her cheeks.

"He's gone again," she said quietly. She actually seemed sad about it.

"Don't cry, Mama—we ought to celebrate," I told her. I meant it.

Mama smoothed my hair. "I worry about you, honey. That you'll think all men are like your Daddy. But they aren't. Grandpa never treated Grandma that way. And years ago your Dad was a kind and thoughtful man. Do you remember those days?"

"No," I said. I didn't want to believe her.

"That was before Amber, Dee-Dee and Christopher were born," Mama said. "Supporting a family of seven is a lot of responsibility for one man to handle. And having to work two jobs has been hard on him."

"You're just making excuses," I said angrily and stalked into the laundry room.

As usual, the hamper was full. I opened the cupboard to get more detergent to start another load and found a whiskey bottle. My blood ran cold. Was Mama a secret drinker?

I shoved it back in the cupboard, afraid to think about what that half-empty bottle of amber liquid meant.

When summer vacation came around, Mama started working full time. Our neighbors, the Boyds, moved out and another family moved in. They had a teenaged son named Eric, who was tall, with wavy dark hair and a killer smile. He was only a year older than me, and soon we became friends.

Eric would come over after Mama went to work and usually didn't leave until just before she came home. Amber went to day camp, and Bobby would disappear for hours on end, hanging around with his friends. I'd send Dee-Dee and Christopher out to play, and Eric and I would play house. It was fun. We talked about what we wanted in a house. I told him all the conveniences I wanted. He helped me wash dishes and fold laundry.

After about a week, Eric started bringing over a couple of his parents' beers and we'd sit on the couch and drink them. "Our own happy hour," he told me. I liked the taste, and I knew I could handle it. We'd been doing this for about a week when, after our second beer, he put his hand on my breast.

"You feel nice—soft," he told me.

"Don't do that," I said, and slapped his hand, jumping up from the couch.

"Why are you so mad?" he asked, sounding totally confused.

"Because you're just like every other man! There's only one thing on your mind."

"Can you blame me? Come here," he said, and led me to the bathroom, making me stand before the medicine cabinet's mirror. "Look at yourself. You're beautiful."

"No, I'm not."

"Yes, you are," he said and turned me to face him. "You have beautiful blue eyes and blonde hair. And you've got a great body. I'd be crazy if I wasn't madly in love with you."

"In love?" I asked, surprised.

"Yeah."

Then he leaned forward and pressed his warm full lips against mine.

I wasn't sure what I was feeling, but when Eric kissed me again, I didn't want him to stop.

Soon we were back on the couch kissing and fondling one another when Chris came in from outside. I buttoned my blouse and hurried into the kitchen. Eric played video games with him for a while before he had to go home. And as I started making supper, I kept thinking about the new intimacy we'd shared.

Soon Eric and I were doing more than just necking when the little ones went out to play. Eric bought a package of condoms at the drug store and together we learned how to use them.

I was afraid Bobby would tell Mama about Eric and me, but Eric swiped some of his mother's cigarettes and bribed Bobby to keep quiet.

When the school year began, Mama went back to working just evenings, and Eric and I would make love in Mama's bed after I put the kids to sleep.

Eric made me feel so special. He made me feel loved, something that I hadn't felt in a long time—maybe never.

We made plans for the future. In a year or so Eric would go work at his father's used car lot, and he'd get me a job there, too, as the firm's secretary. Then we could be together all the time.

Everything was perfect until I missed my period in October. I kept waiting for it to come, and as every week went by I got more and more scared. I told Eric, but he said not to worry. We'd always used condoms and everybody said they worked ninety-eight percent of the time.

In early November, I bought a pregnancy test and sat in the bathroom and cried when it came out positive.

How could this have happened to me?

Bobby banged on the door. "Hurry up! I'll be late for the bus. Mama, Emily's hogging the bathroom!"

"Emily—" Mama called.

I opened the door and ran for my bedroom. Dee-Dee was still on the bottom bunk, playing with her dolls, and Amber was getting dressed for school. I threw myself on my bed and cried.

"Mama, Emily's crying," Amber yelled down the stairwell.

Mama came charging into our room. "What on Earth's gotten into you?" she asked.

"I feel sick. I can't go to school today," I said.

"Well, then go back to bed for a while," she said and took the girls downstairs.

I cried for most of the day, and when Mama went to work that night, I called Eric on the phone. "I'm pregnant," I said.

"You can't be."

"Oh yeah—do you want to see the pregnancy test?"

"It has to be wrong. We used protection every time."

"What if one of the condoms had a leak in it? What if—"

"I'll buy another test. The one you had was probably defective."

But when I took that test it, too, came out positive.

"Shit," Eric spat, sounding a lot like my father. "This is gonna screw up my entire life."

"What about my life?" I cried.

"Hey, you knew the risks."

"What are you saying?"

"That if you tell anyone it was me who knocked you up, I'll deny it. I'll tell them you're a tramp—because that's what you are!"

With that, he flew out of the house, slamming the door behind him.

I'd never felt so lost or alone. And I felt so ashamed. I'd made the same mistake as my mother. By wanting to feel loved, she'd ended up pregnant far too many times. Having Amber, Dee-Dee, and Christopher had not only ruined her marriage, but it had ruined her life.

I didn't want that to happen to me.

The kids were in bed when Mama came home. I was all set to tell her, but she was obviously exhausted and made a beeline for the booze. She was drinking heavily these days—saying it was the only thing that relaxed her.

I went to bed and cried myself to sleep.

The next day, I used the pay phone at school to call the local family planning center to make an appointment for an exam, then skipped out to keep it.

"Yes," the doctor told me, "I'd say you are at least eight weeks pregnant. What do you want to do about it?"

There was only one decision I could make.

"I want an abortion."

The doctor shook her head sadly. "Are you sure?"

I nodded, tears flowing down my cheeks. I told her about Mama and Daddy's separation—and how both them were drinking—and our whole dysfunctional family. I told her about Eric, too. Then she told me about my rights.

In our state, minors could have abortions without their parents' permission, but she urged me to talk to Mama about it. She even offered to do it for me, but I shook my head.

"Mama would be so ashamed of me," I said. "And she works so hard to support us. I can't ask her to take on yet another responsibility."

"There's always adoption," the doctor suggested, but I'd already made up my mind.

I made an appointment to have the abortion the next day and skipped out of school again.

Afterward, I came home as though nothing was wrong. I had awful cramps and just wanted to be left alone, but Bobby wouldn't watch the kids and somebody had to do it.

Even though I was exhausted, I couldn't sleep that night. I remembered the joy I felt when I'd first held three-day-old Amber. Silent tears burned my eyes. I had ended my own baby's life. It was the right decision, but I knew it would haunt me for the rest of my life.

Finally, I cried myself to sleep, vowing that I'd never have sex again. But I also dreamed about Eric, the way his hands caressed me, the way he made me forget about my crummy life. He had truly made me feel beautiful.

I got detention for skipping school, and Mama was angry with me when I wouldn't tell her how I'd spent the day.

"You're grounded," she said, but since I had to help out around the house and never went anywhere anyway, it wasn't much of a punishment.

Daddy showed up the next evening, and I worried that he'd somehow found out about my guilty secret. He'd always seemed so big, so strong, so invincible, but that night he looked pale, his face gaunt.

"Bobby, you watch the kids, I want to talk to your mother and your sister," he said tiredly. Mama looked frightened as he sat us down at the kitchen table.

"I've got heart problems," he said without warning, and Mama gasped. "I've been having chest pains for a while now. Probably all the stress of working two jobs for so long."

Mama bit her lip and looked guilty, like it was all her fault they'd had so many kids—why he'd needed to work so much. Had she forgotten how freely he'd spent for all of his toys?

"I need surgery," Daddy said. "And afterwards, I'll need time to recover. I want to come home."

"Of course you can," Mama said and reached out to hold Daddy's hand.

"Why can't your friend Cheryl take care of you?" I asked.

Daddy's face reddened, but instead of yelling, he put a hand on his chest and took a shaky breath.

It wasn't guilt I felt, but anger that he'd use his illness to try to gain our sympathy.

"When can I come home, Janet?" he asked, turning sad eyes on Mama.

"Tonight, tomorrow. Whenever you want," Mama said.

They talked for half an hour more, making plans, but I couldn't listen. I went up to my room and beat my fist against my pillow.

Finally, I heard Daddy's car take off, and Mama brought the girls upstairs to put them to bed.

"Why are you letting him come back?" I asked her, tears still stinging my eyes.

Mama handed Dee-Dee her favorite doll and tucked her in, then turned to me.

"When I got married, I promised to take care of your father in sickness and in health. Right now he needs us."

Funny how he never needed us when he was driving his boat, or going away on hunting weekends, or screwing around with his girlfriend.

Daddy had heart surgery the next week. I spent the day at school—afraid he would die, but also afraid he would live and insist on being a part of our lives forever. Mama was at the hospital the whole day, holding his hand when he awoke from the anesthesia. He was back living with us in a matter of days.

At first, he was listless and, if we were quiet, he'd leave us alone, preferring to lie on the couch and watch TV for hours on end. Mama quit work to take care of him, and for a couple of weeks, I didn't see as many whiskey bottles in the recycle box.

That didn't last, either.

As Daddy began to feel better, he began to drink again. And even though he wasn't well enough to go back to work, he would disappear for long hours during the evenings—probably visiting his girlfriend, I realized. He and Mama would fight, and Daddy would clutch his chest and tell Mama she'd be the death of him.

Still, it took two long months before Daddy moved out again. With no real skills, Mama had to find yet another minimum wage job—this time at a fast-food joint.

She'd only been working a couple of weeks when the phone rang early one evening.

"Is this Emily Miller?" a voice asked.

"Yes."

"My name is Sergeant Hodges, with the Gardener Police Department."

The blood in my veins seemed to freeze. "Is something wrong with my mother?" I said, sensing bad news.

"She was involved in a car accident. The paramedics have taken her to Mercy Hospital. You were listed as her next of kin."

I sank into one of the kitchen chairs, not knowing what to do next. The officer gave me the hospital's number, but upon hanging up, I called grandma in Ohio instead.

"Oh, sweetie, Grandpa and I will be there by morning. It's all right, Emily. It'll be all right," she promised.

But it wasn't.

I sat looking at the silent phone. There was nobody nearby I could call to take me to the hospital, and I was determined not to call Daddy. He'd probably yell at her and cause a scene. She didn't need that. She needed someone to be with her, and I felt terrible that I couldn't do it.

I did call the hospital and was relieved when they said her condition was stable.

I didn't sleep that night, making irrational contingency plans. I could drop out of school and go to work, but I knew Mama would never let that happen. I could find a job on weekends. Even ten or twelve hours of minimum wage dollars would help support us. I wouldn't be able to buy new clothes, shoes, or nail polish, but the kids would have cereal and milk. It could work.

The next afternoon, Grandpa took Bobby, Amber and me to the hospital to visit Mama. She looked at us, and tears filled her swollen, blackened eyes. Her mouth worked, but she couldn't seem to speak. I held her hand, but her fingers didn't curl around mine.

"It's okay, Mama, I'll take care of the kids until you get home," I promised. I hoped she'd understood my unspoken plea for her not to let Daddy reenter our lives.

Grandma had other ideas.

"That's your father's responsibility," she said sternly. "And it's about time he lived up to it."

She stalked out of the room.

We were still there when Daddy showed up an hour later. His face was red with anger. "Why wasn't I called sooner?" he demanded, and his shouting upset Mama, who started to cry again. The nurse threatened to send hospital security to drag him out if he didn't quiet down.

I pulled Grandma out into the hall. "Why did you call him?" I demanded.

"Because he's your father."

"Sperm donor you mean," I said.

Horrified, Grandma slapped my face, hard. "Where did you learn to talk such filth?"

"I'm not a child anymore, and I haven't been for years." I

looked toward Mama's room, where Daddy stood blocking the doorway. "And that man hasn't got a clue how to be a father."

The doctor arrived and ushered the family into a conference room to talk about Mama's condition.

"Her injuries were relatively minor, but she hasn't responded well to treatment. She's malnourished, and I've ordered a mental exam. She seems clinically depressed."

Daddy listened grimly.

"Is my Mama gonna come home soon?" Amber asked the doctor.

"Pretty soon," he promised, as we left the room.

A uniformed officer waited nearby to talk to the doctor.

"What's he here for?" I asked.

The doctor's expression darkened. "I'm sorry to have to tell you, but at the time of the crash, your mother's blood alcohol was double the state limit."

Oh my God! Mama had been drunk at the time of the crash! Why hadn't anyone told me?

Daddy moved back into the house that night—and Bobby ran away. How I envied him, but it left me having to deal with Daddy by myself, and take care of the rest of the kids, too. It turned out Bobby had only gone to stay with his friend, Gordon, and Gordon's parents offered to keep him for a couple of weeks until things settled down.

Mama was supposed to be released from the hospital and arraigned on Friday, but the phone rang on Thursday evening soon after visiting hours had ended.

Daddy looked pale as he hung up. "Your Mama just died of heart failure," he said.

I stood there at the kitchen counter, making the kids' school lunches for the next day, not believing what I had just heard.

"She can't be dead—she was supposed to recover. The doctor said so."

"I've got to call the funeral home," Daddy said and headed for the shelf where Mama kept the phone book.

"Wait a minute—aren't you going to tell Amber and the others? What about Grandma and Grandpa?"

"You can tell them," he said.

Stunned, I left the jelly-smeared counter and practically stumbled up the stairs to the kids' bedrooms, wondering how I would ever tell Amber, Dee-Dee, and Christopher that their Mama was never coming home.

I gathered them in the girls' room, seating them on the bottom bunk, fighting back tears.

"Remember the story Mama used to tell us about how angels protect those they love. Those who need them most?"

Three blonde heads nodded in agreement.

"The angels came for Mama tonight."

"Did they have wings?" Dee-Dee asked.

"I—I think so," I said, fighting the urge to cry.

The youngest two couldn't seem to grasp the fact, but Amber understood too well. Without a word, she climbed into the top bunk, holding her favorite doll, and just rocked for hours on end.

I climbed up there and held her for a while, but I really didn't know what else to do for her—I needed comforting, too—so I left her alone and called Grandma and Grandpa, who were still at a nearby hotel. Grandma burst into tears and it was then I realized that I hadn't allowed myself to cry for my own mother.

By that time, I couldn't.

I had no tears left.

The next two days were a nightmare. Bobby came to the funeral parlor, but he wouldn't look at Mama in her coffin or speak to Daddy. I heard a couple of our neighbors talking in hushed tones.

"I asked the nurse," Mrs. Taylor said, shaking her head. "She said Janet should have made a full recovery."

"Then why did she die? Was it hospital negligence?"

"No. Janet willed herself to die because she didn't want to live." Mrs. Taylor looked toward Daddy. "And who could blame her."

After the funeral, Grandma begged Daddy to let us to go live with her and Grandpa in Ohio. I prayed that Daddy would say yes, but of course, he didn't.

"They're my kids and they belong with me."

That was the end of the discussion.

That night I faced Daddy, feeling terrified, but determined to speak my piece. He sat at the kitchen table, staring at nothing.

"There have to be new ground rules if we're all going to live here together," I said to him as he sipped his coffee laced with whiskey.

He looked up at me, contempt curling his lip. "What are you talking about?"

"You may be our father, but your behavior is no longer acceptable in this house."

His eyes narrowed, but I didn't let him interrupt.

"Our mother is dead because you treated her shabbily. You hit her, you cheated on her, you let her work—and drink herself—to death, all because of your own selfishness.

"You had a boat, but she never had a dishwasher. You went bowling, and she never went out at all—unless it was to work. You treated her like a punching bag, but you will never hit one of us, or I will have you arrested."

Daddy pushed his chair back from the table and stood, towering over me. "Who the hell do you think you are, talking to me like that?"

I met his steely gaze and didn't back down.

"Janet Miller's daughter."

In that moment I knew I was stronger than Mama had ever been, standing up to the brute who'd made her life—and the lives of her children—a living hell for so many years.

For the first time in my life, I saw Daddy back down. He looked away and then sat down, staring at the worn Formica tabletop for long minutes. He suddenly looked old, and I realized that despite the operation, he had not regained his health. Finally, he got up, went into the living room, sat in his chair and watched television for the rest of the evening, though he didn't seem to be taking it in.

I washed and then folded laundry.

It felt like I'd spent most of my life folding laundry.

Mama's death changed Daddy. He was still an incredibly selfish man, but he didn't yell quite so much. Bobby never lived with us again. Daddy told Social Services he couldn't control Bobby, who was placed in foster care. I almost envied him, because the people he went to live with were nice. They even had a cake on his birthday and invited the kids and me over. Bobby had his own room, in a clean house with new furniture. His foster parents even talked about helping Bobby go to college someday.

Despite Daddy's more subdued attitude, he still made our lives miserable. Without Bobby to protect him, Chris became the focus of most of Daddy's rages. He'd pick on Chris when I wasn't home, and my baby brother's once quiet disposition changed to that of an angry, surly boy.

For the next year, I went to school and took care of the house and the kids. But on graduation day I came down to the kitchen and faced Daddy once again.

"I'm leaving."

Daddy glared at me.

"I'm eighteen now and no longer a minor. It's Amber's turn to help with Dee-Dee and Christopher."

"Where will you go?" Daddy asked. He didn't seem angry, just annoyed, because I was about to inconvenience him.

"My school counselor got me a job as a live-in nanny. God knows I've had enough experience."

"Your mother wouldn't like this," he said. He always said that when he wanted me to do something, but I'd had enough of guilt.

"I'm only taking my clothes. They'll pick me up tonight."

Daddy didn't say a word, just finished his coffee and headed out the door for work.

That was the last time I ever saw him.

Amber burst into tears when I told her. She knew what my leaving meant. I'd protected her and the other kids from our father's rages all their lives. But I was tired. I felt like I'd never felt a moment of joy in my life. It was killing me to leave them, but I needed to save myself. I hoped that if I could earn enough money I could rent an apartment big enough to take care of us all. It was a pipe dream, but it was that thought that kept me going.

I tried to keep in touch with Amber, but she refused to talk when I called. She blamed me for dumping the responsibility of taking care of Daddy, the house, and the other kids on her. I couldn't make her see that after ten years, I'd earned a life of my own. Despite this, I felt miserable. I had promised Mama I'd take care of the kids and I'd failed her.

To soothe my conscience, I got the county welfare people to check on them and make sure Daddy wasn't physically abusing them.

Amber left home at seventeen, leaving fifteen-year-old Dee-Dee to handle the house—and Daddy. Chris got mixed up with the wrong crowd at school. Daddy didn't want to deal with him and had him shipped off to a foster home, too.

Chris didn't make out as well as Bobby. He ran away countless times and ended up in a juvenile facility. I blamed myself but wondered if things would have been any different if Mama had lived or if I'd stayed at home.

Chris's problems only reinforced my own resolve to make a better life for myself. I took computer classes in the evenings and got a job in an office. It was there I met a wonderful man named Joe Renner. He was everything Daddy never was—kind and gentle—and when I met his parents, I instantly liked them. I could see that his father was a good man who loved his wife and children and that Joe would be the same kind of husband and father.

We were married the next spring. Dee-Dee begged me to invite Daddy—and forgive him. She insisted that he'd changed, but I didn't believe her.

Mama's five children were reunited for my wedding, and for a day, at least, we were happy.

Daddy had a fatal heart attack later that summer. It was up to me to make his final arrangements. I decided to make it simple. I had his remains cremated and asked the others if they wanted a ceremony. Only Dee-Dee said she'd come. Of course, the funeral parlor was full of Daddy's beer-drinking, fishing buddies. They all called him a great guy and said how they'd miss him. A couple of hard looking women showed up—Daddy's ex-girlfriends?—but neither Dee-Dee nor I spoke to them.

None of us went to the cemetery for the internment.

A few months later, I was heartbroken to receive a call one Sunday morning, informing me that had Chris had died just hours before of a drug overdose.

Once again it was me who arranged—and paid for—the funeral. I hadn't seen Bobby in several years, but he showed up in a suit and tie, accompanied by a pretty young woman he introduced as his fiancée. We all gathered at the graveside to place red roses on Chris's grave. Joe and I left half a dozen yellow roses on Mama's grave, too.

Dee-Dee came to live with Joe and me and stayed for a couple of years. We helped her pay for junior college, and she got a good job and met her own Prince Charming.

I've got my own kids now, a boy and a girl, and our home life is nothing like what I grew up in. When I look at them, so innocent and sweet, I often think about the baby I never had, and wonder what he or she would have been like.

These days I see Bobby, Amber, and Dee-Dee as often as I can, and am pleased that four of Mama's children have good lives, and hope that poor Chris has a least found peace. It took Amber years to finally forgive me for leaving the family. And it was with great guilt that she confessed she felt the same longing for freedom when she, too, left Dee-Dee and Chris with Daddy. That spirit of forgiveness has brought us even closer.

Just about every day I think about Mama and wish she could have lived to see—and know—her grandchildren. But at least I know that the cycle of abuse my father started has been broken and that Bobby, Amber, Dee-Dee and I will never let violence and selfishness corrupt our own families.

Chapter Two

COLD CASE

by L.L. Bartlett

"You're not the first psychic to come through Paula's apartment, Mr. Resnick."

Hands on hips, Dr. Krista Marsh stood before me. Her heels gave her an inch or more on me. Blonde and lithe, and clad in a turquoise dress with jet beads resting on her ample breasts, she was the best-looking thing in that lower-middle-class apartment.

"I don't use that term. Con-artists, liars, and frauds take advantage of people with problems. I'm just someone who sometimes knows more than I'm comfortable knowing."

Truth was, I hadn't wanted to be there at all, giving my impressions on the fate of four-year-old Eric Devlin. He'd gone missing on an early-autumn evening some eight months before. One minute he'd been there—riding his Big Wheel in front of the apartment building—the next he was gone. Like every other good citizen, I'd read all the stories in the newspapers and seen the kid's picture on posters and on TV. The only place I hadn't seen it was on the back of a milk carton.

I was there as a favor to my brother—actually, my older half-brother—Dr. Richard Alpert, who'd joined me on that cold gray evening in early May. Richard was Paula Devlin's internist at the university's low-income clinic. He liked Paula and hated how not knowing her son's fate was tearing her apart. He hoped I could shed some light on the kid's disappearance.

I'm not sure why Dr. Marsh was there. Maybe as Paula's therapist, she thought she could protect her patient from someone like me.

So, there I stood, in the middle of Paula's modestly furnished living room, trying to soak up vibes that might tell me the little boy's fate.

Paula waited in the doorway, looking fearful as I examined the heart of her home, which she'd transformed into a cottage industry, distributing posters, pins, and flyers in the search for the boy —all to no avail. Vacuum cleaner tracks on the carpet showed her hasty clean-up prior to our arrival. Too thin, and looking older than her thirty-two years, Paula's spirit and her determination to find her missing son had sustained her over the long months she'd been alone. The paper had never mentioned a Mr. Devlin.

"I don't know if I can help you," I told Paula.

She flashed an anxious look at Richard, then back to me.

"Where would you like to start, Mr. Resnick?"

"Call me Jeff. How about Eric's room?"

A sixty-watt bulb illuminated the gloom as the four of us trudged down a narrow hallway. Paula opened the door to a small bedroom, flipped a light switch, and ushered us in. "It's just the way he left it."

I doubted that since the bed was made and all the toys and games were neatly stacked on shelves under the room's only window—not a speck of dust. A race car bedspread and matching drapes gave a clue to the boy's chief interest—so did the scores of dented, paint-scraped cars and trucks. I picked up a purple-and-black dune buggy, sensing a trace of the boy's aura. He'd been a rambunctious kid, with the beginnings of a smart mouth.

"He was a very lively child."

"He's all boy, that's for sure," his mother said proudly.

She hadn't noticed I'd used the past tense. Either that or she was in deep denial. I'd known little Eric was dead the moment I entered the apartment.

I gave her a half-hearted smile and replaced the toy on the shelf. There wasn't much else to see. I shouldered my way past the others and wandered back to the living room. They tried not to bump into each other as they followed.

A four-foot poster of Eric's smiling face dominated the west wall. He'd been small for his age, cute, with sandy hair and a sprinkle of freckles across the bridge of his nose.

An image flashed through my mind: a child's hand reaching for a glass.

I hitched in a breath, grateful my back was to Dr. Marsh. A mix of powerful emotions erupted—as though my presence had ignited an emotional powder keg. Like repelling magnets, guilt and relief waged a war, practically raining from the walls and ceiling.

Composing myself, I turned, a disquieting depression settling over me.

"Ms. Devlin—"

She stepped forward. "Call me Paula."

"Paula. Did Dr. Alpert tell you how this works?"

"He said you absorb emotions, interpret them, and that sometimes you get knowledge."

"That's right." More or less. "There's a lot of background emotion here. May I hold your hand for a moment? I need to see if it's coming from you, or if it's resident in the building."

Without hesitation, she held out her hand, her expression full of hope. And that's what I got from her: Hope, desperation, and deep despair. She loved that little boy, heart and soul. And there was suspicion, too, but not of me.

I released her hand, let out the breath I hadn't realized I'd been holding.

"Paula, ever heard the expression about a person taking up all the air in the room?" Her brows puckered in confusion. "You're broadcasting so many emotions I can't sort them out. I know you want to stay, but I can't do what I have to if you're here."

"But he's my son," she protested.

Dr. Marsh stepped closer, placed a comforting hand on Paula's shoulder. "You want him to give you a true reading."

I turned on the psychiatrist. "I'm not a fortune teller, Dr. Marsh."

"I didn't mean to offend," she said without sincerity.

"I'll go if you say so, Krista." Paula grabbed her windbreaker from the closet and headed for the door. Once she was gone, my anxiety eased, and I no longer needed to play diplomat.

"What're you getting?" Richard asked.

"The kid's dead—been dead since day one. He wasn't frightened either, not until the very last minute."

"You're talking murder," Richard said. "Not Paula."

"No. I'm sure of that."

Dr. Marsh eyed me critically, brows arched, voice coolly professional. "Are you well acquainted with sensing death, Mr. Resnick?"

"More than I'd like." I glanced at Richard. "What's this about a pervert in the neighborhood?"

His eyes narrowed. "It hasn't been reported in the media, but Paula told me about the cops' prime suspect. A convicted pedophile lived three units down at the time the boy disappeared. They've had him in for questioning five or six times, but haven't been able to wring a confession out of him. How'd you know?"

"From Paula—just now. She's afraid he took her kid."

Dr. Marsh frowned. She probably figured I was just some shyster running a con. Can't say I was sorry to disappoint her.

"You got something else," Richard said. He knew me well.

"I saw something, but it doesn't make sense." I told them about the vision.

"Close your eyes. Focus on it," he directed.

I shot a look at Dr. Marsh, saw the contempt in her gaze. Skepticism came with the territory.

My eyes slid shut and I allowed myself to relax, trying to relive that fleeting moment.

"What do you see?" Richard said.

"A kid's hand reaching for a glass."

"Is it Eric?"

"I don't know."

"Describe the glass."

I squeezed my eyes tighter, trying to replay the image. "A clear tumbler."

"What's inside?"

"Liquid. Brown. Chocolate milk?"

"Look up the child's arm," Richard directed. "Can you see his clothes?"

The cuff of a sleeve came into focus. "Yeah."

"The color?"

I exhaled a breath. Like a camera pulling back, the vision expanded to include the child's chest. "Blue...a decal of—" The image winked out. "Damn!"

"Give it a couple of minutes and try again," Richard advised.

Uncomfortable under Dr. Marsh's stare, I wandered into the kitchen again. I couldn't shake the feeling of...dread? Whatever it was surrounded me, squeezing my chest so I couldn't take a decent breath.

Hands clenched at his side, Richard studied me in silence. We'd been through this before, and his eyes mirrored the concern he wouldn't express for fear of embarrassing me. He knew just what these little empathic forays cost me.

Turning away from his scrutiny, I went back into the boy's gloomy bedroom. Though banished from the apartment, Paula's anguish was still palpable. How many times had she stood in that doorway and cried for her child?

I ran my hands along all the surfaces a kid Eric's age could've touched. After eight months there was so little left of him. His clothes in the dresser drawers, neatly folded and stacked, bore no trace of his aura. I pulled back the bedspread, picked up the pillow, closed my eyes and pressed it against my face. Tendrils of fear curled through me.

Airless.

Darkness.

Nothingness.

Death.

A rustling noise at the open doorway broke the spell. Dr. Marsh studied me as she must've once looked at rats in a lab. Her appraising gaze was sharp, her irritation almost palpable. Even so, she looked like she just walked off the set of some TV drama instead of the University's Medical Center campus. I'd bet her brown eyes flashed when she smiled. Not that she had.

"I understand you've done this before," she said.

"Define 'this,'" I said.

"Helping the police in murder investigations."

"Once or twice."

"Are you always successful?"

"So far," I answered honestly and replaced the pillow, smoothing the spread back into place.

"And what do you get out of it?"

Her scornful tone annoyed me.

"Usually a miserable headache. What is this, an interrogation?"

"I'm merely curious," she said. "My, we are defensive, aren't we?"

"I can't answer for 'we,' but I'm certainly not here to fence with you, doctor. If you'll excuse me."

Brushing past her, I headed back to the kitchen. The smooth walls and ceiling were practically vibrating. Eric's childish laughter had once echoed in this room, though nothing of him remained there. I frowned; I still didn't have the whole picture, and Dr. Marsh had rattled me.

I opened all the cupboards. The remnants of Eric's babyhood —plastic formula bottles and Barney sippy cups—had been stowed on the higher shelves.

No Nestle's Quik.

"Any conclusions?" Richard asked.

"Whatever I'm getting seems strongest in the kitchen." I leaned against the counter, stared at the refrigerator covered with torn-out coloring book pages attached with yellowing Scotch tape. Something about it bothered me. I opened the door.

Paula wasn't taking care of herself. A quart of outdated skim milk, half a loaf of sliced white bread, a sagging pizza box and three two-liter bottles of diet cola looked lonely in the full-sized fridge. No chocolate milk. An opened box of Tater Tots, a sprinkling of damp crumbs, and a couple of ice trays were the only things in the freezer. Everything looked completely innocent, yet something was terribly wrong.

"Do you think all the apartments are set up the same?" I asked Richard.

He shrugged.

Pushing away from the counter, I walked through the rooms one last time—just to make certain—then paused in the kitchen before heading into the building's entryway. No trace of Eric, but something else lurked there.

Hands thrust into her jacket pockets, Paula waited by the security door, looking pale and frightened. I couldn't even muster a comforting smile for her.

"Chocolate milk," I said.

She blinked.

"Did Eric drink it?" I pressed.

"He loved it but was allergic to chocolate. I never had it in the house."

I glanced up the shadowy staircase. A wounded animal will

always climb. Eric hadn't been wounded, but something had lured him up those stairs. I took three steps and staggered against the banister when a knife-thrust of pain pierced the back of my head —fierce, but unlike the skull-pounding headaches, these intuitive flashes usually brought.

"You okay?" Richard asked, concerned. Was he feeling guilty for roping me into this?

I leaned against the wall, closed my eyes and tried to catch my breath. "Who lives upstairs?" I asked Paula through gritted teeth.

"Mark and Cheryl Spencer in apartment D. A retired widow, Mrs. Anna Jarowski, lives on the other side."

"Did they see Eric the day he disappeared?"

Paula shook her head. "No."

I took another step. The heaviness clamped tighter around my chest. I'd felt something when I first entered the building, but I'd assumed it belonged to Paula.

I'd been wrong.

"I want to talk to them."

"They've been cleared," Paula insisted.

I didn't budge.

She bristled with impatience. "You came here to find answers about my son, not waste time questioning my neighbors. They've been cleared by the police and badgered by the press."

"Paula," Richard said gently. "It can't hurt."

Finally, she tore her gaze from mine, stormed back to her apartment, letting the door bang shut.

Richard took the lead, leaving Dr. Marsh and me to follow. He went to knock on the first apartment door, but I shook my head. He gave me a quizzical look and I nodded toward the opposite door.

Richard crossed the ten or so feet to the adjacent door and knocked. We waited. Were Richard and Dr. Marsh struck by the unnatural quiet in that building?

The door opened on a chain. Steel gray no-nonsense eyes peered at us. "Yes?"

"Mrs. Jarowski, I'm Doctor Alpert and this is Dr. Marsh," Richard said with authority. "We're from the University. May we speak with you?"

Mrs. Jarowski blinked in surprise. "Did Dr. Adams send you?"

Dr. Marsh gave Richard an inquisitive look, but he said nothing.

Mrs. Jarowski looked at us with suspicion. "Can I see some identification?"

"Of course," Richard said, and reached into his coat pocket.

"I left mine in my purse," Dr. Marsh said.

Mrs. Jarowski scrutinized Richard's hospital security badge. "Please come in," she said at last.

I didn't want to. I wanted to go home. I wanted to be anywhere but this place that smelled of mothballs and sour cabbage.

She ushered us inside, stepping into her kitchen. Anna Jarowski was a compact woman in her mid-sixties. Her short silver hair was caught back from her forehead with a barrette, like something out of the 1950s. Dressed in a faded housecoat, no makeup brightened her wan features, leaving her looking colorless and ill.

She glanced at me. "I'm sorry, but I didn't catch your name."

"Jeffrey Resnick," I said, forcing a smile, and shoved my hand at her.

The woman eyed my outstretched hand, hesitated, then took it.

Our eyes locked. Her hand convulsed around mine. Peering past the layers of her personality, I looked straight into her soul.

A tremor ran through me. I pulled back my hand, my legs suddenly rubbery. Sweat soaked into my shirt collar and I took a shaky breath, hoping to quell the queasiness in my gut.

"Do you mind if I sit?"

She gestured toward the couch in the living room, but I lurched into the kitchen and fell into a maple chair at the worn Formica table. The others followed, leaning against the counters, looking like wallflowers at a dance. Mrs. Jarowski moved to stand in front of the refrigerator, arms at her side, body tense. The open floor plan allowed me to look into the apartment. Like the kitchen set, the rest of the furniture was shabby but immaculate. Mrs. Jarowski's faded housecoat was freshly ironed. She probably spent her days scrubbing the life out of things.

I looked around the sterile kitchen, an exact replica of the room directly below us—the floor, the counters, the cupboards—everything, right down to the white plastic switch plates. Three embroidered dishtowels lined the oven door pull, Mrs. Jarowski's only concession to decor. The tug of conflicting emotions was even stronger than downstairs. We looked at one another for a few moments in awkward silence.

Mrs. Jarowski cleared her throat. "Are you a doctor, too?" she asked me.

"You might say I'm an expert on headaches. Tell me about yours, Mrs. Jarowski. Migraines, aren't they?"

The old lady's sharp eyes softened. "I've had a lot of tests, even a couple of CAT scans, but they've all been inconclusive. I've been told they're due to stress. One doctor said they're psycho-somatic."

"I doubt that," I said, winning a grateful nod. "They get pretty bad sometimes, don't they?"

She nodded again, looking hopeful.

"I can sure identify with that. I got mugged last year. A teenager with a baseball bat cracked my skull. Since then I get some really bad ones. I'm working up to a doozie right now."

"What does that have to do with me?" she asked, an odd catch to her voice.

"Nothing. Tell me about Eric Devlin."

Her back went rigid. "I've already told the police, I don't know anything about his disappearance."

"His mother said he was 'all boy,' but I get the feeling he was a little hellion. A noisy kid. Kind of a brat, really."

Dr. Marsh glared at me as if I'd blasphemed God Almighty. The whole city had developed a reverence for the missing child.

Mrs. Jarowski didn't share that feeling.

"He used to ride up and down the sidewalk on one of those big plastic tricycles for hours at a time. Up and down and up and down. They make one hell of a racket, don't they?"

Her lips tightened. The tension in that kitchen nearly crackled.

My nausea cranked up a notch and I loosened my tie. On the verge of passing out, I rested my elbows on the table to steady myself.

"When I have one of these sick headaches, I have to lie down in a dark room with absolute quiet. Otherwise, I think I'd go insane. That ever happen to you?"

Mrs. Jarowski's gaze pinned me.

The vision streaked before my mind's eye: Eric, eyes round with anticipation, his small hand clutching the tumbler of chocolate milk, something his mother would never let him have. Paula calling to him from somewhere outside. The half-empty glass falling to the spotless floor, shattering. Chocolate milk splashing the walls and cabinet doors.

"It's peaceful and quiet these days," I said. "Like a morgue." My gaze drifted to the full-sized refrigerator—back to her. I swallowed down bile. "Do you want to show me?"

Her cheeks flushed. She wouldn't look at me.

Dr. Marsh and Richard looked at me in confusion. Mrs. Jarowski seemed to weigh the question, her solemn gaze focused on the floor.

"The freezer, right?"

Mrs. Jarowski's anger slipped, replaced by a tremendous sense of guilt—but not, I noticed, remorse.

"Dr. Alpert, maybe you should have a look."

She held her ground.

Richard brushed past me, crossed the room in three steps. His eyes bored into hers and she backed down, moving aside. The freezer door swung open. A heavy, black plastic garbage bag filled the space. He worked on the twist tie, pulled back the plastic. His breath caught and he slammed the door, suddenly pale.

"Holy Christ."

The quartz wall clock ticked loudly, but time seemed to stand still.

At last, Richard moved to the phone and punched 911. "I'm calling to report a body at 456 Weatherby, apartment C."

Richard swallowed as he listened to the voice on the other end of the phone. Dr. Marsh blinked in confused revulsion.

Stony-faced, Mrs. Jarowski turned, her slippered feet scuffing across the vinyl floor as she headed for the living room. She sat down on her faded couch, picked up the remote control and turned on the television.

Finally, Richard hung up the phone.

"Dr. Marsh, can you watch Mrs. J until the police get here?" I asked.

She nodded, still looking shell-shocked.

I squinted up at Richard. "Maybe you could help me to the bathroom. I don't want to barf on Mrs. J's nice clean floor."

Breathing shallowly, I sat back against the lumpy couch, a hand covering my eyes to blot out the piercing light. After more than an hour, two of my pills still hadn't put a dent in the throbbing headache.

The cops had already taken Mrs. Jarowski away. The ME

arrived, and the crime photographer was still flashing pictures in the kitchen. The place was full of cops, and the murmur of a dozen voices drilled through my skull.

"Can I get you something, Mr. Resnick?" Lieutenant Brewer of the Buffalo Metropolitan Police stood over me. The chunky, balding cop still seemed taken aback that his case had been broken by an outsider.

I squinted up at him. "Yeah. Assure my privacy—don't give the press my name. The last thing I want is publicity."

"Okay, but answer me this; how'd you know?"

"I don't know how it works, it just does."

"The old lady waived her rights. Said she heard Ms. Devlin had signed a new two-year lease and decided she'd had enough of the noise. She lured the kid up here and made him quiet —permanently."

"And the chocolate milk?" Richard asked me.

"The lure of a forbidden treat. Mrs. J ground up sleeping pills, had him drink it," I said. "When he was dopey, she planned to smother him."

I thought about it—remembered what I'd seen when I'd touched her. Fury gave her the strength to hold the boy, who'd struggled in those last minutes. She'd sealed his nose and mouth with a wad of freshly pressed linen dishtowels, pinning him against the floor until his body slackened, his small chest no longer heaving. Then she'd heard Paula Devlin frantically calling for her son. Anna Jarowski sat beside the dead boy for a long time —triumphant in the knowledge she'd finally silenced her intolerably noisy neighbor.

I looked up at Brewer. "I take it you haven't searched the place yet."

"Call me paranoid, but I'm waiting for a warrant. No way do I want this thrown out on a technicality."

"You'll find what's left of the tricycle in one of the closets.

She's got a hacksaw. Been cutting it up and sneaking it out in the trash for the past eight months."

Dr. Marsh elbowed her way through the crowd in the kitchen. She'd been gone about an hour—breaking the news to the boy's mother, no doubt.

"How's Paula?" Richard asked.

"I gave her a sedative. Now that her mother's here, I think she'll be all right." She looked at me. "How are you, Jeff?" Her icy veneer had melted, her best bedside manner now firmly in place.

"Sick."

"But you've got to feel good about what you've done."

I frowned. "I made two women miserable. Why would that make me feel good?"

She seemed puzzled by my answer, but I didn't have the energy to explain it to her. "Dr. Marsh, you said another psychic came here—what did she tell Paula?"

"That the boy was well and living in a small town down South, anxious to be back home with his mother."

Poor Paula.

"Do you need me anymore?" I asked the detective.

He shook his head. "Go home before you keel over."

I glanced at my brother. "Now would be a good time, Rich."

I moved on shaky legs. Richard and Dr. Marsh steadied me on the stairs. We ducked under the crime scene tape and they pushed me through the throng of press as we headed for Richard's Lincoln Town Car.

Dr. Marsh crushed her business card into my palm. "Call me." Her voice was husky, excited, like a rock star's groupie.

Reporters and cameramen swarmed as she slammed the car door. Richard left her to deal with them, taking off with a squeal and leaving rubber on the asphalt.

"Sharks," he muttered.

I leaned against the headrest and considered my first consultation. By all counts, a royal success.

Then why did I feel so dirty?

Did Jeff make that call to Dr. Marsh? What happened to Paula Devlin? Find out by reading the fourth Jeff Resnick novel **BOUND BY SUGGESTION.**

In exchange for helping her unlock the emotions of a disturbed young woman, psychiatrist Dr. Krista Marsh promises to cure Jeff Resnick's recurring headaches via hypnotism. Things start out rocky and quickly get worse when both the young girl and the doctor begin to manipulate Jeff. Soon he's experiencing the young woman's emotions and can't tell where hers leaves off and his begin, and Krista has other reasons for ingratiating herself into Jeff's life. Meanwhile, Jeff's brother Richard is vying for a chairman seat on the hospital's fund-raising board. Two seemingly unrelated events that suddenly converge with deadly results.

Read: ***Bound By Suggestion***

Chapter Three

AN UNCONDITIONAL LOVE

by Lorraine Bartlett

I suppose I looked out of place at the wake. My tight, black cocktail dress was molded to my fanny like a second skin, but Kathryn would have thrown her arms around me in an enthusiastic hug, glad to see me if I'd shown up buck naked. That's the kind of friend she was.

Losing a good friend like Kathryn is like losing a piece of your soul. How was I going to get through my week without our Monday lunchtime gabfest? We'd met a couple of years before at a basket-making class. She'd taken it as a lark, a way to excise stress, but it was the start of a part-time business for me. We remained friends after the course ended.

Kathryn owned a dress boutique and knew the ins and outs of running a small business in a trendy part of town. Her advice was worth more than gold. But starting a company takes time and money. Working a full-time secretarial job paid my living expenses, but I hustled drinks at night to earn capital to expand my business.

Kathryn's sudden death had shaken me. A rainy night, slick pavement, and a drunk driver. She was only thirty-seven.

Because we didn't travel in the same social circle, I didn't know anyone else at the wake. These gatherings always resemble a cocktail party; the only things missing are the finger foods and the guest of honor.

The tall, mustachioed man at the head of the receiving line was laughing—remembrances of happier times, no doubt—but his eyes betrayed the depth of his loss. That had to be Marty, Kathryn's husband. I'd never met him, probably never would, I thought as I skipped the line and wandered the room, avoiding the white casket. Why in God's name did it have to be open? The waxen-faced husk in the satin-lined box bore no resemblance to the vibrant woman I had known.

Two tiers of flowers, at least thirty arrangements, surrounded the casket and lined the far wall. I read the cards. Business associates, friends, and family. Some were touching: *My darling wife. I'll love you always. Marty.*

For our baby girl. Life will never be the same without you. Mom and Dad.

I wiped at a tear. How awful to outlive your child.

I couldn't read any more.

Someone had assembled a haphazard collage, and I stopped to look at the dozens of pictures. Kathryn's vibrant smile brought a lump of grief to my throat. I didn't recognize any of the other people in the pictures—except for her husband. I glanced across the room. Yes, just as she'd described him: tall, handsome, a full mustache touched with just a hint of gray, and mesmerizing blue eyes. But now, dressed in the dark suit of mourning, he looked colorless—wan. Kathryn knew how to pick clothes. Had she chosen them for Marty, too? On some other occasion, he'd look sensational in that three-piece suit.

I studied the photos. Vacation shots at the Grand Canyon; Kathryn in her garden, at the opening of her shop, childhood school pictures, and in her wedding gown. She'd told me that she and Marty were childless, although not by choice. They were still trying to decide if they should adopt when she was killed. In the meantime, she'd thrown herself into making her shop a success, but she'd always talked about her joy-filled times with Marty. Now who would he have to share his days and the lonely nights ahead?

I glanced at my watch. I'd told my boss at The Half-Time that I'd only be gone an hour. I didn't bother to sign the guestbook or introduce myself to any of Kathryn's family. I'd come for her —not them.

Back at the bar, the night dragged. Maybe it was the steady drizzle or the realization that my friend was forever gone, reinforcing my own sense of mortality. Or was it the knowledge that if something happened to me there'd be no throng of friends and family to mourn my passing. I'd always been a loner. When Tony and I broke up three years ago, I'd retreated. Lost touch with old friends, shied away from making new ones.

Except for Kathryn.

Caring for my invalid mother had caused the breakup of my marriage. After mother died, I was truly alone. I'm sorry to say that I hardly missed her—or the threats of hell and damnation she'd showered on me since I was a small child. She'd never have approved of my working at the bar. It was only Kathryn's friendship that kept me going during those first lonely months. That and her steadfast encouragement. She praised my work, sold my first pieces in her shop, and convinced me I could not only make a living but be a success in the business world.

I hefted a tray of drinks and delivered them to a party at a table near the kitchen. Glasses clinked, a toast was made and suddenly I prayed there'd be a designated driver in the group. A drunk driver had taken my only friend from me. How ironic that I should work in a place where people drank themselves into an unconscionable irresponsibility. But the tips were good, I rationalized. Another year or two and I could quit my day job. Until then, I needed to build my inventory and make business contacts.

It was nearly eleven when Marty walked in and took a seat at the bar. Why, of all places, had he shown up at this beer joint? Had he gotten in his car and just driven, stopping at the first—or last—place he came to?

Jim, the proprietor and bartender, gave Marty a shot of whiskey and he downed it, ordered another, then stared vacant-eyed at the TV and the late newscast.

My shift was over. I probably should have minded my own business and gone home to my lonely apartment, but seeing that forlorn figure hunched over a glass, I felt I should at least offer my condolences.

"Marty. Marty Prescott?" I said.

He turned his troubled gaze toward me.

"Hi, I'm Leslie—a friend of Kathryn's."

He studied my face for a few moments. "You were at the funeral home."

I nodded. "Kathryn and I were good friends. We met at the community college."

"That's right. She mentored you with your business."

"Yes."

"You work here?"

I nodded.

He signaled to the bartender. "Another round, and one for the lady."

"Sorry, sir, but I'm afraid I can't serve you any more."

"I only had a couple. I'm still sober."

I could tell he wasn't. He probably hadn't eaten anything all day—which is why the alcohol hit him so hard. He was just looking to deaden the pain, which wasn't going to happen.

"I'd be happy to call a cab for you," Jim said.

"I could drive you home," I offered without thinking.

"I don't need—" Marty went to stand and pitched forward, falling against the bar. I reached to steady him, but he pulled his arm away.

"What about my car?" he asked.

"You can pick it up tomorrow."

He thought it over.

"Believe me, pal, you don't want to risk a DUI," Jim added.

Swallowing his pride, Marty nodded and followed me to my car.

The drive was silent. I glanced across the bench seat, but Marty kept his gaze focused out the rain-dotted passenger window.

I pulled up the drive, and Marty spilled from the car. I followed him up the steps, watching as he fumbled with his keys.

"Can I help?" I asked.

Embarrassed, he handed them over to me. I opened the door, letting him in first.

He flicked on lights as he went through to the kitchen. "Can I get you something?" he asked.

"I don't think so," I said, feeling odd in my dead friend's house —alone with her husband. "I'd better go."

"Please, don't. I—" he faltered. "I don't want to be alone right now."

Indecision filled me. Were the neighbors watching? What would they think?

Who cared what they thought. The man was alone—really alone. And I wasn't cold-hearted enough to ignore another human being's pain.

"Okay. But just for a few minutes."

He reached into one of the cabinets, took out a couple of wine glasses, then grabbed an opened bottle from the fridge. He stared at the label. "Kathryn opened this on Friday. She wasn't much of a drinker, but she enjoyed a glass with dinner." He chewed at his bottom lip, and I thought for a moment he might cry.

"Shall I pour?" I asked.

He nodded, trying, unsuccessfully, to hide his haunted expression.

I poured the wine, handing him a glass. He wandered through

the house, turning on lamps and the stereo. Soft music filtered from the speakers.

The house was immaculate, but tables and the mantle seemed devoid of decoration. The basket containing silk flowers that I'd made for Kathryn as a thank-you gift for all her advice, took center stage on the cocktail table.

"Most of our framed pictures are at the funeral home. Makes the house seem so empty," Marty explained.

"Have you made any plans?"

"My brother advised me not to rush into anything. He said that I should live here for at least a year before I even think of selling. But I don't think I can stay. Everything here reminds me of her."

He cleared his throat. "Thanks for driving me home. It was pretty foolish of me to go to a bar. But I couldn't take another minute of well-meaning platitudes from our friends and family. So where do I go? A bar. The bartender was right. What if I'd had a few too many? What if I'd caused an accident and killed someone else's wife or child?" Emotion twisted his features.

"Don't torture yourself," I soothed. "You've suffered enough."

"Kathryn was trapped in the car for over an hour, conscious part of the time. She knew she was dying. My god, is there anything crueler?" His voice broke and he looked away.

"You've had to deal with too much in too short a time. And you've got a difficult day ahead of you tomorrow. You should get some rest. Is that the bedroom through there?"

He nodded,

He let me take his arm, lead him into the darkened room. I turned on a bedside lamp, then helped him with his suit coat. He fumbled with the buttons on the vest, struggling out of it, then started on his shirt.

"I'd better go," I said, as I finished hanging the garments on a hanger.

"Wait," he said, touching my shoulder.

I hesitated, felt the room charge with tension.

I met his watery gaze. "Thank you," he whispered.

We stared at one another, then suddenly I was in his arms, his hungry kiss smothering my mouth. Caught up in the moment, I returned the kiss with as much urgency.

Before I knew what was happening, we were on the bed—Kathryn's bed—he was pulling at my dress, and I was fumbling with the zipper on his pants, both of us captured in the passion of the moment.

It was the roughest, but most satisfying sex I'd ever experienced. And at the moment he climaxed, he called out, "Kathryn," in a slow, painful wail.

He collapsed on top of me. His ragged, wine-laced breaths were warm on my neck. I held onto him as his body was wracked with shaking sobs.

He'd made love to Kathryn, not me—I was just a body double. But for some reason, I didn't feel hurt—only ashamed that I'd given in to the animal passion that had seized me.

After a while, his choking breaths steadied, and he rolled away from me. Soon his breathing steadied and he slept.

Careful not to disturb him, I eased off the bed, grabbed his pants, went through his pockets and found his keys. In the dim light, I grabbed my own clothes and crept away from the bedroom, dressing in the hall before slipping out the front door.

I drove back to The Half-Time, retrieved Marty's car and drove it back to the house. I slipped inside again, left his keys on the kitchen table, and pulled the locked door behind me.

The rain had stopped and the autumn air was crisp. The mile or so walk gave me plenty of time to berate myself the way my mother would have. *Tramp. Harlot. Fornicator.* Those were just a few of the words she would have used to describe me.

No! I protested. I'd done the right thing—helped ease another's pain.

Then why did I feel so cheap?

I awoke late the next morning. By the time I got up, Kathryn's funeral was already underway.

I called in sick, which wasn't too far from the truth. Heartsick.

The memory of Marty's tortured eyes haunted me as I sipped my coffee. He hadn't been sober and I knew alcohol lowered one's inhibitions. Maybe he wouldn't even remember making love with a virtual stranger. He didn't know my last name—would he even remember my first name? Had I ever given Kathryn one of my business cards? I didn't think so. His car was in his own driveway —maybe he would convince himself our tryst had never even happened, or that it was only an alcohol-induced dream.

Still, they say confession is good for the soul, and I needed to unburden myself. But to whom? No one at my mother's church....

Kathryn, of course.

I waited until late that afternoon before driving to the cemetery. The caretaker gave me directions to the newly dug grave. The earth was mounded, the ground festooned with many of the flowers that had been at the funeral home the night before.

Marty's red roses were prominently displayed.

"I'm sorry, Kathryn," I whispered. "I didn't mean to do it—no way would I hurt you. Please don't blame Marty. He wasn't making love to me—it was you he wanted, you he cried out for. You left such a hole in his life...."

The entire speech sounded stupid. Kathryn was dead. Beyond knowing—or caring—what had happened between Marty and me. She might not hold it against me, but I knew I'd feel shame until the day I died.

I stood for a long time just staring at the fresh grave, knowing I could never receive Kathryn's forgiveness.

When I got home, I found the light flashing on my answering machine.

"This is Deborah Wilson, the buyer at Monroe's Department store. I'm sending you a purchase order, but wanted to confirm on the phone our intention of ordering fifty of your deluxe baskets for our gourmet shop. Please call me to confirm a delivery date."

I couldn't believe my good luck! On Kathryn's advice, I'd taken samples of my prettiest, most complicated baskets and given a dog-and-pony show at Monroe's downtown office. More elaborate—and expensive—than what they could obtain from China, these baskets were truly unique. I'd have to work day and night for weeks, but if I could deliver them on time, I'd be rewarded with more orders.

I grabbed the phone and punched in the familiar number, excited to share my happy news.

"You have reached Kathryn's Dress Boutique. The owner has passed away and the shop will be closed. Please direct all inquiries to—"

Devastated, I hung up the phone, collapsed into a chair and cried my heart out—for my friend, but mostly for myself.

I worked day and night to complete the Monroe order, even taking three vacation days. They were ecstatic over the baskets and rewarded me with another order. For the first time, I was glad I had no social life, determined to make my business a success.

Everything seemed to be falling into place. Within two months, I felt confident enough to quit cocktail waitressing for good. Orders were coming in for more baskets all the time, and I even considered hiring a couple of the other women who'd taken the same class with Kathryn and me.

Within that same period of time, I also knew I was pregnant. I hadn't been with anyone except Marty for a very long time. There was no way I was going to intrude on his life. He'd had enough heartache. And though I still felt guilty about that night, this pregnancy wasn't a problem for me. My biological clock had been ticking—very loudly—for some time. I'd even considered artificial insemination until I looked into the cost. I had no love interest but I longed for a child—just as Kathryn had.

To live with myself, I convinced myself it was Kathryn's last gift to me. The child she could never have—the one she and Marty so desperately wanted. Still, that thought couldn't erase the guilt I felt surrounding my baby's conception.

I busied myself, working at my business and preparing for my baby's birth. Everything would be perfect. My own father had died when I was an infant, and my mother had been both parents to me. My baby and I would have to carry on the same way. And we'd make it. I was determined not to repeat the mistakes my own mother had made. My child would always know how much she was loved. No one would ever cause her pain.

My pregnancy was uneventful, and I carried my sonogram photos, showing them to anyone who'd look. I joined an expectant mothers group, shopped for my little girl's layette, and counted the days until her due date.

It was nine months to the day of Kathryn's death, and I was in the doctor's waiting room for my scheduled appointment when my water broke. Within an hour, I was admitted to the hospital and assigned a birthing suite. My labor lasted only twelve hours when I heard my doctor telling me to push—really push.

"Here's the head," Dr. Stewart announced cheerfully.

It wasn't as bad as I thought it would be. I'd had a charmed pregnancy and an easy labor. Everything continued to be perfect.

"Push," the doctor ordered.

Intent on my breathing, I didn't notice how quiet the delivery room had become.

"One last push," Dr. Stewart coaxed.

I ground my teeth and pushed with every ounce of strength I had.

"It's a girl," she confirmed, and I heard the weak mewing of a newborn.

"Let me see her, let me see her!" I cried joyfully.

"We need to clean her up," said one of the nurses tersely.

I still wasn't done with my own work and lost track of time until after I delivered the placenta.

A nurse wiped sweat from my face. "Where's my baby? Where's Anne Kathryn?" I asked.

Her gaze shifted across the room to the doctor.

"Dr. Stewart?" I asked, fear suddenly swelling inside me.

"We're still checking her out. There's a bit of a problem."

My heart constricted in fear: was she saying my baby wasn't perfect?

She moved to the bedside, patted my hand. "Don't be alarmed. It's a common birth defect. And the good news is it isn't life-threatening, and it can be repaired."

"What's wrong with her?" I cried.

"The baby has a cleft lip and palate."

A scrubs-clad nurse stepped forward and settled the pink-blanketed bundle into my arms. Nothing prepared me for that first sight of my daughter. Where part of her nose and perfect lips should have been was a gaping hole.

My breath caught in my throat as tears sprang to my eyes. Quickly I handed her back to the nurse.

"Dear God, why me?" I cried, looking into the obstetric nurse's patient face. She gazed at the swaddled bundle in her arms, made no comment, but her expression said it all. God hadn't punished me—he'd punished Anne because of me!

The nurse took the baby away and I buried my face in my pillow. Dr. Stewart jabbered on about the miracles of plastic surgery, but all I could think of was the malformed face on that otherwise perfect child.

I couldn't stop crying and Dr. Stewart gave me a sedative. I must've slept, but when I awoke, newborn shame filled me. I had rejected my own child—hadn't even tried to bond with her. All my perfect plans were gone. I wasn't even going to be able to breastfeed her.

I had produced a hideous creature. That innocent child had been cursed at the moment of her conception because I'd had intercourse with my dead friend's husband.

Dr. Stewart arranged for me to talk to a therapist, but shame continued to burn through me. No way could I confess the true source of my guilt. So I listened and nodded my head and vowed to myself that my daughter would always be my top priority.

I was released from the hospital a day later. Anne Kathryn had her first surgery at ten days old. Two days later, they sent her home.

Despite her disfigurement, Anne cooed and fussed like any other infant, and in only days, I fell in love with her.

I hadn't really been prepared to take care of a normal, healthy child. Taking care of a handicapped one offered challenges I'd never expected.

Feeding her was an ordeal. I'd never even heard of nasal regurgitation and was unprepared to deal with it. I joined a support group. They gave me feeding tips and stressed that a cleft palate couldn't be traced back to anything the mother had done wrong during pregnancy. These things just happened. Sometimes clefts ran in families.

I knew little about my own extended family—and nothing about Marty's. It was just a fluke of fate. Not a punishment. But I couldn't get rid of the guilt. I'd have to just live with it. Maybe that, too, was my punishment.

Finding competent daycare took up most of my maternity leave. The cost was more than I could afford. Welfare was a tempting alternative, but I was determined not to be a burden on society. My basket-making business folded almost immediately; I couldn't meet the orders and ended up selling my inventory at a loss. Waitressing was out of the question, too. I traded in my car for an older model, found a smaller apartment, downscaled my entire life.

Those first couple of years were hard, caring for a handicapped child and working full time. But Anne was a joy to me. Thank God for my sympathetic boss and supportive co-workers. They collected money for Anne's periodic surgeries, each operation bringing her incrementally closer to looking more like a normal child.

But her deformity was so severe, chances were she'd never look completely normal. I worried about how her peers would treat her. The Internet was full of stories chronicling the cruelty of children and well-meaning but thoughtless adults. I wouldn't be able to shield Anne forever. Together we had to learn to steel ourselves against the scrutiny of strangers.

I'd lay awake nights wondering if one day I should tell her about her father. I wasn't about to intrude on Marty's life. Lying was the easiest solution. More guilt, another sin, but if it saved Anne pain, then that's the way it had to be.

It was early evening and I'd just picked Anne up from day care when I realized I'd run out of milk. I stopped at the grocery store and decided I'd pick up a few other items, too.

Turning my cart into the dairy section, I literally crashed into another shopper.

"I'm sorry," I began but stopped as I recognized the handsome, mustached man standing before me. Marty Prescott. I hadn't even seen him since the night of Anne's conception.

"Excuse me," I stammered and made to hurry past, but he caught my basket.

"I know you, don't I?"

"I don't think so, I—"

"Yes. You were Kathryn's friend." He had to think about it for a moment. "Leslie, right?"

"And you're Marty."

He looked down at Anne in the grocery cart's child seat. "And who's this?" he asked, stepping around to see my daughter's face.

I prepared myself for his reaction. After three years, I'd heard every cruel question, thoughtless comment, but he stared in horrified silence at her misshapen nose and lips. Anne's surgeon had done a magnificent job—but more years of reconstructive surgery still lay ahead.

"Cleft palate," I said unnecessarily.

"Yes," he said, the color draining from his face.

He kept staring at her. Anne smiled, offered him her toy. "Beanie," she cried in delight.

He forced a smile. "Beanie," he agreed.

He looked into my eyes. His mouth worked, but no sound emerged.

"Yes, she's yours," I blurted, instantly regretting it. "I've always thought of her as the child Kathryn could never have."

"Never wanted," he said bitterly.

I blinked in surprise. "What?"

He stroked his mustache. "She asked me to grow this. I was born with a cleft lip. Kathryn didn't want to take the chance of having a child with the same condition. I couldn't blame her—but I assured her we'd love any child we had together. Kathryn wasn't so sure." He let out a shaky breath. "At least she was honest about it. To cope, she threw herself into her work. She wouldn't even consider adoption."

That wasn't the way I'd heard it. Had Kathryn told me a more socially acceptable story, one to garner sympathy? What else had she lied about?

Suddenly the crystal pedestal I'd always put her on began to fracture.

"Excuse me," said another shopper, trying to inch her cart around us.

Marty moved aside. "This isn't the time or place, but we need to talk. Would you...have coffee with me?"

I glanced at my watch. "I really don't have time tonight. Anne's scheduled for surgery tomorrow morning and, I—"

"I understand," he said, cutting me off. "Maybe some other time?"

I took my time answering. But there was something in his eyes, a longing maybe, that caused me to stammer, "Sure." I gave him my number, hoping he'd never call.

That night as Anne slept I studied her peaceful face. I hadn't realized how much she resembled her father. The same mesmerizing blue eyes. Had she received her sunny disposition from Marty, too? I'd only met him in stress-filled situations.

The next morning I sat in the lonely surgical waiting room, a new tie-dyed bunny—Anne's after-surgery reward—in my lap. The wait for news from her surgeon was nerve-racking. Everything would go fine, I reassured myself. I'd trusted Dr. Weinstein on so many previous occasions. He'd promised me that Anne would go to her prom, and reminded me that all brides are beautiful. Anne would be, too.

I tossed the well-thumbed magazine aside and glanced at my watch. Another hour or more to go.

"Can I join you?" asked a male voice from the doorway.

Marty held a bouquet of pink daisies in one hand, and a bakery sack in another.

"I thought you might be hungry. My mother used to treat herself to a jelly doughnut while she waited for me to come out of surgery."

I choked back my surprise and anger. Anger?

Yes, anger.

"You don't owe us anything," I said sharply. "I never intended to tell you. I never expected help—"

"I realize that. You're a nice woman who treated me kindly when I was in mourning." He took the chair across from me in the otherwise empty waiting room. "I've thought about that night so many times. Couldn't believe it happened, that I'd betrayed my marriage vows...."

What could I say in my own, or his, defense? I kept silent, couldn't look him in the eye.

"It couldn't have been easy for you," he continued.

No. It hadn't. But then, what good was wallowing in a pool of self-pity? That wouldn't have been good for me or Anne. The old saying, "you made your bed now lie in it," had become my life's motto. But I'd had a lot to think about since our brief conversation the evening before. Had I really known Kathryn? In my mind, I'd made her a paragon of virtue when she was only flesh and blood, just like me.

And Marty.

"You must have made a new life," I said.

"Made a mess of my life," he said. "After the funeral, I started drinking. Never had an accident, thank God, but things got pretty bad for a while. I alienated my friends, nearly lost my job. Then I joined Alcoholics Anonymous. I've been sober for two years."

Did he want my approval? What else could he want from me?

"I'm glad for you," I said cautiously.

"And now I've been blessed with the most unexpected, and terrific news; I have a daughter. I know we're practically strangers, but...I'd like to get to know her, and you. I know what she's going to go through. I can help."

I searched his earnest expression. Did I believe him?

"That's very kind of you, but—"

But what? There was really no reason to rebuff his honest attempt to get to know us.

"Thank you," I finished lamely.

"Leslie?" Dr. Weinstein stood in the doorway.

I met him in two steps.

"It went faster than I thought. Anne came through fine. She's in recovery and is asking for her new toy," he said, smiling.

Marty was suddenly at my side. The doctor's gaze shifted to take him in.

"This is Marty Prescott, Anne's—" I nearly choked on the word, "father."

Dr. Weinstein's eyes widened, but he made no comment.

"I'm due back in surgery. You can see Anne in an hour or so. I'll have the nurse come get you."

"Thank you, doctor."

I watched him go.

"Thanks, Leslie," Marty said sincerely, "for that introduction. I'd like to be a real father to Anne."

My insides felt shaky, and I groped for a chair. "You're pushing too hard, Marty. Maybe you'd better go."

"But—" He stopped himself, crestfallen. He seemed to steel himself. "If that's what you want. For now. But I'll be back. I promise."

He turned and headed down the corridor. I fingered the cellophane around the cheerful daisies. Anne would like them.

I pursed my lips, afraid to admit to myself that I liked them.

Marty was as good as his word and showed up that evening for visiting hours, arms loaded with beanie toys—much to Anne's delight. We didn't talk much—it was still too awkward. When it was time for him to go, he shook Anne's hand.

"We're friends now, right?"

Anne looked at me for confirmation. I nodded.

"Friends," Anne tried to say through the swath of bandages. She hugged her new stuffed kitty.

Anne was asleep before visiting hours ended. I slipped out of the children's ward and headed for the exit. Marty was waiting.

"Can we have that cup of coffee now?" he asked.

"You don't give up easily," I said.

"Not when I have so much at stake. I'd like us to be a family."

"That's an awfully tall order," I said. His mustache drooped, the skin around his eyes creasing in fine lines. "Why don't we try friendship, first?"

His expression lightened, and he managed a shy smile.

I honestly didn't believe that Marty and I had a chance together. It seemed pointless to even hope. And yet in the days and weeks that followed, Anne fell in love with her daddy.

And, I was afraid that I might be falling in love with him, too.

We'd been going out for almost six months and on a snowy afternoon found ourselves at the local mall, sitting on an oak bench, waiting to buy tickets for the afternoon kiddy matinee. Anne sat on Marty's lap, stroking the hairs of his mustache. "Can I see your scar?" she asked.

Marty glanced at me, and then swallowed before turning back to our daughter. "Why?"

"Because it makes us the same. You can see mine," she said, her voice sounding oh-so-solemn as she fingered the raised line that ran from her nose to her lips, "Why can't I see yours?"

Marty looked away, and for a long moment, he stared down at the floor. Then I saw him swallow. "If you want me to, I'll shave off my mustache. But I want you to know that I wouldn't do it for anybody but you, baby."

Anne's deep blue eyes bore into Marty's for a long time, then she shook her head. "You don't have to. I just wanted to see if you would."

"I will if that's what you want," he assured her.

I held my breath, and for a moment, I thought both Marty and I might cry.

Small Anne shook her head. "Nope. You don't gotta." She ducked her head and spoke quietly to me. "Mama, this one's a keeper."

I stared at my daughter, open-mouthed. Where on Earth had she ever heard that phrase?

Anne still has a number of surgeries to go, but she's gorgeous in her mom and dad's eyes. And three months after our movie date, she was beautiful in a lacy pink dress, a circlet of daisies gracing her hair, spreading petals as the flower girl at Marty's and my wedding.

Chapter Four

WE'RE SO SORRY, UNCLE ALBERT

by Lorraine Bartlett

Until we put him in a convalescent home, my family had no idea Uncle Albert was worth a fortune.

"I could just kill the bastard," Uncle Leo said, his gray mustache quivering, brown eyes flaming.

A glance around the big mahogany-veneered table in the cramped dining room told me he wasn't the only one of the relatives who felt that way.

Aunt Donna poured coffee from the glass carafe as those assembled passed around the sheaf of papers outlining Uncle Albert's net worth: over a million dollars. No one in the family wanted to take care of the old man after he'd fallen and broken a hip, so until he could take care of himself, he'd been sentenced to St. Anne's Home.

"Mandy, why didn't you tell us about this sooner?" Leo thundered.

"I knew it would cause a lot of trouble." Which it had. Even more, if Uncle Albert found out we all knew about the money. I'd discovered his healthy bank balance after he'd asked me to bring his checkbook to him at the home. I'd also found a copy of his will, his monthly Merrill Lynch statement, and other financial papers tucked away in his desk.

"All these years," Uncle Leo, Albert's brother, rumbled, his face purple, "that miserable skinflint mooched off us. Hanging around for meals, borrowing tools and never returning them. Never even offered a nickel toward his own mother's funeral."

"Not a birthday card or even a kind word," Aunt Donna chimed in, settling her broad bottom onto the chair at Leo's left. It was three weeks before Christmas and she looked just like Mrs. Santa Claus in her silver-framed glasses and gingerbread-cookie print apron.

"Why did Uncle Albert call Mandy and not one of us?" Ricky challenged in his best bully voice. As the oldest of the cousins, he always tried to manipulate us—but I hadn't surrendered since age twelve when he'd guilt-tripped me into loaning him my Monopoly game, then saying it was his.

"Mandy was always his favorite," Dawn, Ricky's sister, piped up, her perpetual whine as grating as ever. I still bristled when I remembered that not only had she sided with Ricky, as usual, but had used that whine to ask why I gave Ricky the game and not her.

"It doesn't matter. We're all treated the same in Uncle Albert's will," I reminded them. "Even though, so far, I've had to do all the work. Like finding him a space at St. Anne's, taking care of his escalating demands—and visiting him, too."

Leo clasped the copy of the will in his meaty fist. "The question is what are we going to do about it?"

"What can we do?" Donna asked, meeting his gaze.

Leo glared at her. "The longer Albert sits in that nursing home, the less money there is for all of us."

Ricky's eyes narrowed. "You're not really thinking about killing him off, are you, Dad?"

I blinked in astonishment. Talk about a leap in logic!

"The sonuvabitch deserves it," Leo said, and reached behind

him to the sideboard, taking out a bottle of rye and pouring a generous amount into his coffee. He set the bottle on the table with a thunk. Good old Uncle Leo—he found the solutions to all his problems in a bottle.

"Now, dear," Aunt Donna said, patting Leo's shoulder. "I'm sure you don't mean that. Although...." Her voice trailed off and she looked wistful.

All eyes were riveted on her perfectly powdered, wrinkled face. I reached down to grab the purse from my lap, rearranged its contents, and placed it on the table.

"What are you thinking, Ma?" Ricky demanded.

"Well, just how much that money could mean to the family. Kathy and Ted..." she glanced across the table at my older sister and her husband, "...could pay off their boat. Dawn has that second mortgage, and Mandy has all those school loans. Leo and I have never had a real vacation. It would just be nice if the family could benefit from all that money."

"Instead, it'll be the damned nursing home," Ricky growled. What kind of debt had he accumulated? Maybe the Harley, the Lexus, and clothes that never said "off the rack."

"We don't know that for sure. Once his hip heals, he could be home in a couple of months," I said. "His mind's still as sharp as a tack. If he lost weight, the doctors say he could live another ten years."

"He'll outlive us all," Uncle Leo complained, taking a gulp from his coffee mug.

"I think we should just do it," Dawn said, her voice cold.

All eyes turned on her.

"Kill him?" Kathy said, aghast. "How?"

"We could hire somebody," Dawn said.

"Don't be stupid," Ricky said. "How do you know the person you hire isn't gonna be some undercover cop?"

"Then *we* should do it." Dawn reached for her huge handbag and pulled out a soft-covered book. "It wouldn't be that hard. I saw this in the bookstore. It tells you everything you need to know."

She passed around the maroon-colored book. *Death: A How-To Guide for Writers*. Had she, too, been considering murder before this little impromptu meeting?

Ricky flipped through the pages. "That's too easy," he said, his gaze pausing momentarily on the subhead "poisoning," before passing the book along.

"This kind of talk is all nonsense," Aunt Donna said.

"Not necessarily," Ted said. Lanky and nondescript, my brother-in-law tended to fade into the background. He rarely opened his mouth at family gatherings, and even his wife turned a surprised glance in his direction. "If we planned it carefully, we could do it."

Silence.

"How?" Uncle Leo said at last.

"It would have to look like an accident," Kathy said quietly. Was my Girl-Scout-Leader sister's tone actually cunning?

"That won't be easy. The old fart never goes anywhere—or does anything," Ricky said.

"Then a car accident is probably out of the question," Dawn said, toying with the gold chain at her thin throat.

"The bathroom is the most dangerous place in the home," Donna offered.

"This is crazy," I said. "You can't be serious."

"Hush up, Mandy. You'll get your share," Kathy said.

"Ted's an electrician—he could do something to the wiring," Dawn suggested.

"Sure—water and electricity don't mix. Fry the old bastard," Ricky said, warming to the idea.

Ted looked thoughtful. "It's possible. I'll bet the wiring in Albert's decrepit old house isn't even up to code."

"It's all settled then," Leo said, a note of triumph in his voice, and uncapped the rye bottle once more, offering it around the table. Everyone raised their cups in salute. Everyone but me.

They were crazy.

All of them.

I didn't go with the cousins on their errand of murder. Ted had fixed enough hazardous electrical wiring to easily duplicate what was necessary to *cook* the old man.

Instead, I made a visit to the local police department. A Lieutenant Dan Martin was only too happy to talk to me.

"I have it all on tape," I said, taking out the little recorder I'd switched on at the time of the initial discussion.

"Why did you have this with you?" he asked.

"I use it in my job. I take field notes when I visit building sites for my employer. Then my secretary types them up." I rewound the tape a few feet and punched the play button.

"Twenty-four hundred feet of board lumber, six thousand one-penny nails—"

My own voice broke off, and cousin Ricky's voice came on. "What are you thinking, Ma?"

"Well, just how much that money could mean to the family. Kathy and Ted could pay off their boat—"

The Lieutenant listened raptly, and slowly a smile graced his lips.

I had my own set of keys to Uncle Albert's house. The next day the lieutenant and I made a visit, accompanied by his tech team. The cops collected their evidence and the arrest warrants were issued within the week: conspiracy to commit murder. Needless to say, as I was the only one who'd attended that meeting who wasn't arrested, I was also the one they blamed.

"You sonuvabitch," my sister swore at me over the telephone, after she and Ted had made bail. I frowned at her word choice but got her point nonetheless.

"You can't go around plotting murders," I defended myself. "It's just not right! Especially against a member of the family."

"We all hate him—even you do."

"But I can't condone killing the old man."

"You bitch, you stinking bitch!" she'd screamed, nearly piercing my eardrum.

I let the answering machine take the next three or four calls. And I wondered as the threats piled up if I might be their next intended victim.

The last call was from Aunt Donna. "Of course you know you're not welcome to come for Christmas dinner!" she said and hung up the phone.

Should I call Lieutenant Martin again? No, this was just angry family business-as-usual, every Nichols for himself. Neither Uncle Leo nor Ricky would really hurt me—would they? I couldn't help remembering from years ago Uncle Leo's rye-scented roughhousing, and Ricky being responsible for a series of skinned knees. And Kathy—how could my own sister cut me off after all the times I covered for her while she went out with unsavory boys from the manual arts classes, then kept my mouth shut when she married one?

It was with a heavy heart that I headed for the nursing home that gray and chilly Christmas Eve. Uncle Albert was the only family I had left.

I entered the home with a plastic grocery bag containing a holiday-wrapped box of mixed chocolates hanging from my wrist. Blasts of hot stale air assaulted me as I checked in at the nurse's station.

"I'm here to visit my uncle, Albert Nichols," I told the unfamiliar nurse. "How's he doing?"

While she consulted a chart, I took in the holiday decorations of garland and a tabletop Christmas tree. The sweet smell of chocolate fudge and cookies piled high on a tray by her phone couldn't cover the scent of disinfectant and old people, but I itched to swipe one of the confections anyway.

"Making progress. See if you can convince him to work harder on his therapy. He'll be released much sooner if he does," she said.

"Thanks, I'll try." I gave her a quick wave and headed down the corridor.

The door to the private room was open, and I saw the sweating, obese old man propped up on the bed, watching a "Cheers" rerun on the TV bolted to the wall.

"Uncle Albert?"

He picked up his remote and hit the mute button.

"Mandy! Where the devil have you been?" he demanded. His bloated face was the color of a rotten turnip.

I forced a smile and bent down to kiss his spotty cheek. My lips came away wet and I winced. He even smelled like a rotten turnip.

"Are they treating you well?" I asked.

"They're starving me," he growled. "Doctor says I have to lose at least sixty pounds—maybe more."

"Then don't let them know I brought you this," I said and handed him the two-pound box. As I sat down, he tore into the packaging like a kid on Christmas morning.

"Here, hide this in your purse," he said, handing me the crumpled paper and ribbon. He plucked one of the chocolate covered candies from its brown paper cup, stuffing it into his mouth. "The cops said you're the one who stopped them," he said. No further explanation was necessary.

"I couldn't let them hurt you, Uncle Albert," I explained, taking off my gloves. "But now none of them will even speak to me."

"Bastards. All of them," he declared, popping two more of the chocolate creams into his mouth. "You don't need them. Soon as the cops left, I called my lawyer. Had him write me up a new will

—cutting all of them out! He brought it to me this morning. It's already signed and witnessed. I ought to tell Leo I left every penny to this home. Not that they deserve all my hard-earned savings, either."

Was I mentioned in the new will? I wanted to ask, but I couldn't. Didn't want to look guilty by association, I guess. I shifted on the hard, straight-backed chair, feeling uncomfortably warm in my coat, knit cap, jacket, and boots.

"Mandy," he said through a mouth full of candy, "you saved me from those vultures. You're going to get everything I have—for now." His eyes bore into mine. "I can always change it again—if I have to."

"Oh, Uncle Albert," I protested, with a nervous laugh, "you'll live to be a hundred. You're nearly well, and you'll be going home soon," I patted his damp arm and smiled. I hoped he didn't notice me wipe my fingers on my pants leg afterward.

Oodles of fat at the back of his arm undulated as he picked through the chocolates, comparing what was left with the drawing on the cardboard lid. "You're damned right," he said, made his choice and swallowed, then popped a new one into his mouth.

"Oh, dear. Should you be eating all those at once? Here, let me put it aside for later."

Uncle Albert snatched the box away, glaring at me. "I haven't had anything decent to eat in weeks."

At the sound of a knock at the door, he stuffed the chocolates under the sheet.

"Time for your therapy, Mr. Nichols," said the scrubs-clad nurse.

"I'll be in to see you tomorrow, after church," I said, getting up from my chair, grateful for the chance to escape. I stepped closer to the bed, gritted my teeth, and leaned over to kiss the top of the old man's head. "I love you, Uncle Albert."

He stuffed another bonbon in his mouth. "Mm foo, Mamby," he uttered, his jaws locked by chewy caramel.

"Mr. Nichols," the nurse chided, "are you cheating on your diet again?" She placed his worn slippers on his swollen feet and then helped him from the bed to his walker.

"Bye," I said quickly, unwilling to see his bare bottom should the thin cotton hospital gown flap open. I zippered my coat, pulled on my driving gloves, and headed for the exit.

As I passed by the empty nurse's station, I stared at all the goodies. No one had touched them since I'd come in. And there was poor, hungry Uncle Albert, alone and deprived of comforting holiday cheer.

I looked around—no sign of bullying nurses—grabbed one of the holiday paper plates and piled it with cookies, candies, and fudge, then stole back to Uncle Albert's now-empty room. The chocolates were still under the sheet. I emptied the box into the bedside table's drawer, along with the rest of the contraband, put the box back into the crumpled grocery bag, closed the drawer and high-tailed it for the exit. What harm could a couple of extra little treats do on Christmas Eve?

On the drive home, I realized just how lonely this holiday would be. The relatives—even my own sister—wanted nothing to do with me. So, I ate a microwave dinner, played Christmas carols on my stereo, and watched the Yule log DVD I'd rented. Oh, how wretched to be alone on Christmas Eve!

The next morning, after a church service devoid of comfort or joy, I made good my promise and headed for the convalescent home. The corridors were quiet, although I could hear the distant sound of music—Bing Crosby?—coming from the rec hall. I went straight to Uncle Albert's room, but it was empty, only rumpled sheets and his bedside slippers in view.

Heading back down the hall, I stopped at the nurses' station.

"Hi, I'm Mandy Nichols, here to see my uncle, Albert Nichols, but he doesn't seem to be in his room."

The RN's face froze. "Oh, Miss Nichols, I'm so sorry to have to tell you, but your uncle passed away."

I felt my jaw drop and the color drain from my face. "What happened?"

"He went into a diabetic coma. He was rushed to Emergency but died during the night." She led me to a chair, held my arm until I'd slumped into it.

"Why didn't someone call me?" I murmured, still in shock.

"We left a message on your machine. Didn't you get it?"

I shook my head. "How could this have happened?"

"We don't know, but somehow he snuck into the nurses' station, raided our holiday goodies and...." She let the sentence trail off. "It was just too much for him."

"My goodness," I said.

"There's some paperwork you need to fill out, but you can do that later," she said and launched into a recitation of the next steps I'd have to take, including plans for the disposition of Uncle Albert's remains.

"I'm so sorry this had to happen, ruining your Christmas," the nurse said kindly. "He told us how you'd been cut off by the rest of your family. Is there someone I can call to come get you? A friend perhaps?"

"Thank you, but I think I'll just go home," I said, wiping a tissue around the corners of my moist eyes.

She walked me to the exit. "God bless you," she called after me.

As I walked slowly to my car, head bowed, I remembered that I was now all alone in the world. No relatives to share my sorrow —or Uncle Albert's money.

I couldn't wipe the ear-to-ear grin from my face.

~

LOVE HEALS

by Lorraine Bartlett

Diana Mason strolled down Fifth Avenue, taking in the store windows festooned with cheery Valentine's Day decorations. Pink and red hearts, Cupid with his arrows, and hosts of cherubs flanked candy-filled boxes, greeting cards, diamonds, pearls—all the things Madison Avenue had decreed that a woman could possibly want as tangible proof of her man's love on this, the most romantic day of the year.

Give me a break, she wanted to scream, yet she hungrily drank in the sights.

It wasn't a major-league holiday, like Christmas, but in the adult world, it was bigger than Halloween and certainly Arbor Day. Her hardened, logical mind told her that like most holidays, this one was perpetrated on the masses to cash in on sentiment. But how much meaning could it hold when more than half the world didn't even celebrate the day?

She held tightly to her purse strap, staring at the full-carat solitaire engagement ring in a heart-shaped, red velvet box in the jewelry store window. The carefully placed spot lighting made it sparkle—a contrast to the bleak day.

"Oh, Gary, that's the one," a pretty blonde woman cried,

pointing to the same box. Her companion's eyes were riveted on the accompanying price tag, his complexion going pale.

"Oh, I could just die for it!" the young woman gushed. Her grin was broad and proud.

"We just got engaged," she explained.

Diana forced a smile.

"Congratulations."

"Oh, honey, let's get it right now."

"Well, okay," he reluctantly agreed.

Diana watched as the woman pulled her fiancé into the store, and then she turned away, heading up the block once more.

The icy wind stung her cheeks, but she didn't care. She bypassed the subway station, turned the corner and continued down 42nd Street. Right now she didn't need the press of bodies, the stench of stale subway air, and the rabble of haranguing voices in her ears.

Feeling bad about a certain day on the calendar was just plain dumb, she decided. And it was just her luck to have this, of all days, off from her job. Her depression deepened as she realized how much she missed Rick. No, she didn't miss him. She missed having someone to hold her in the night; someone to be there at the other end of the telephone line when she felt lonely. More painful still was knowing it was self-inflicted. But Rick had wanted a playmate, not a soul mate. Being a realist, she saw no reason to continue a relationship that had no future. And there was no new someone in her life.

Except for Jason.

Diana dodged a couple of panhandlers. Had Amanda Reynolds ever felt lonely? Try as she might, Diana couldn't help but make comparisons with the dead woman. But unlike Amanda, Diana knew she had no hold on Jason's heart, except for gratitude— perhaps friendship.

Eaten-up with cancer, Amanda had been Diana's patient for two long weeks. Her rapid deterioration had been painful for even a trained nurse like Diana to witness. Her once-beautiful features were gaunt, her face twisted with suffering. During that time Diana had come to respect the woman's husband. It was obvious Jason loved Amanda with every part of his being. And although there was no hope, night after night Jason had held Amanda's hand, lovingly stroked her hair, and patiently reassured her.

After the funeral, he had visited the nurses' station on her floor, bringing flowers for the staff as a token of his thanks for the care they had given his wife. His eyes were haunted and Diana had invited him for a cup of cafeteria coffee. Of course, he'd only talked about Amanda. But in the months that followed he had visited Diana one or two times a week until a casual friendship developed between them. They talked about their jobs, compared their favorite authors lists, but one topic always crept into their conversation: Amanda.

Jason wasn't even handsome. Balding, with glasses, and only average height, he looked every inch the high school English teacher, not the epitome of a romantic fantasy. But he had a kind, gentle way, a quiet voice, and an easy manner that encouraged trust. And like a schoolgirl, Diana found herself infatuated with this intriguing man who had loved so deeply.

With every step, Diana found her imagination wandering. What had Jason given to Amanda on Valentine's Day? A single red rose; a book of poetry; perhaps a poem he had written himself. Why not? Even her name—Amanda—meant worthy of love.

Hot tears welled in her wind-burned eyes. *You don't need a rebound relationship*, Diana reminded herself, walking faster. *And neither does Jason.*

Her toes were numb by the time she pushed through the door of her apartment building. Stamping her feet on the cracked tile, she checked her mailbox as she waited for the elevator. Once on board, she punched the button for five, rode the distance staring at nothing—trying to feel nothing.

Entering her loft apartment, she tossed her purse on the

couch, flipped through the bills and junk mail once again. Another wave of self-pity coursed through her. There had been no card in the mail—no note under her door. And oh, how she had hoped there might be.

Drawn to the window, she bit her lip, absently gazed over the snow-dusted neighborhood. Disappointment? Why should she feel disappointed? To be disappointed one had to have expectations, and there was certainly no reason to have expectations. About anything.

Turning her back on the twilight, she was determined to purge all thoughts of Jason.

It was nearly 8 p.m. by the time Diana had finished cleaning her already spotless apartment and ironed a stack of clothes. The phone hadn't rung; nothing had intruded on her solitude.

Restless, she grabbed one of the poetry books she'd recently purchased and sat down at the kitchen table with a glass of Merlot. She opened the pages at random and began to read. With each page she turned, her feeling of loneliness increased, a growing thread of anger flaring within her. The rest of the world was out there celebrating Valentine's Day and here she was all alone, reduced to reading mushy poetry and feeling cheated.

You're alone by choice, some part of her reminded. Cheated? What about Jason? How was he feeling on this, his first Valentine's Day without his beloved Amanda?

Diana's heart ached at that thought. How would Jason feel, deprived of the woman he so desperately loved? The memories of their all-too-brief time together would have to last him a lifetime. Knowing the impact of such a devastating loss made Diana feel ashamed. Here she was hoping Jason would be thinking of her when she hadn't even given any consideration to him. His was a romantic nature. No wonder he didn't want to acknowledge the celebration of love and togetherness.

Yet thinking logically couldn't dispel her sense of frustration.

This isn't like you, she scolded herself, wiping at her eyes. But then, since meeting Jason her world had done a topsy-turvy number on her.

She closed the poetry book and set it aside on the table. She might as well go to bed. But Diana knew she couldn't hide from her feelings in sleep, either.

A knock on her door caused her heart to race. "Diana?" came a familiar voice.

"Jason?" She fumbled with the locks. Trying not to appear too eager, she ushered him in. He looked tired—no—weary.

"I was hoping I might see you. Would you like some coffee, or perhaps a glass of wine?" she offered.

He took off his hat and shrugged out of his coat. "Thank you. Wine would be nice.

She tried not to stare at him as she puttered around her kitchen, grabbing another wineglass from the cabinet and some cheddar from the fridge and crackers from the pantry. Still, she'd caught a glimpse of his eyes, sensing his grief and loneliness. Her own spirits sagged. But, she reminded herself, of all the places he could have gone, he had chosen to visit her.

They settled across the kitchen table and she pushed the plate of cheese and crackers closer to him.

He took a sip of his wine. "I'm sorry to just show up on your doorstep unannounced."

"Don't be silly," she chided him.

"It's been a . . . difficult day," he admitted.

"It's never easy to be alone on Valentine's Day," she agreed.

"My students tried very hard to make me feel—"

"Loved?" she supplied.

He nodded somberly.

"They're good kids, but they can't understand."

Diana wanted nothing more than to comfort him with a hug, or even just to touch his arm in sympathy, but instead, she folded her hands to keep them still. "The trappings of the occasion do tend to emphasize one's emptiness. And platitudes and clichés about loves lost and brighter days don't help much, either."

Again he nodded.

"Maybe all we can do," she continued, "is to feel what we feel and mourn the loss."

He stared into his wineglass. "I wish you could have really known her," he said quietly, not needing to explain to whom he referred.

"It's ironic how fate can bring people together, only to tear them apart," she said. "It's hard to believe that the sorrow you feel will one day fade and you'll remember only the good things about your time with Amanda. What better occasion than Valentine's Day to reflect on those memories?"

His smile was tentative.

"You have a poet's heart, Diana." He was quiet for a moment, and then his expression became wistful. "We shared a night of dancing light. Amanda lit over a hundred candles all around our apartment. She'd bought almost as many roses, their scent permeating every room. And she wore a dress of antique lace. When I think of her, I try to remember her as she was on that night."

Diana smiled pensively, feeling not quite as cynical as she had earlier in the day. She'd been right; this day meant more to Jason than cards and candy. "That's a beautiful memory."

His smile held more than a hint of sadness. "Yes, it is."

His brown eyes locked with hers, seemed to study her. She smoothed her long, auburn hair, wished she'd put on a blouse and skirt rather than a sweatshirt and jeans. But then, she hadn't expected a visitor.

The silence grew heavy.

"I've ... I've always thought Valentine's Day was more a cele-bration of commercialism than love," she said. "After all, lovers and friends can always say what they feel on any day of the year," she paused, and then continued, "but I wonder, without this one special day, how many would say what they really feel."

"What do you feel, Diana?"

His question—and the intensity of emotion behind it—startled her.

In an instant, she weighed the consequences of answering honestly.

"I'm lonely. And I worry about you. I hope one day you'll find another someone like Amanda."

He seemed to consider it. "It's been almost a year—a long, lonely year—since I lost her." For a moment, his face was filled with an anguish that wrenched her soul.

He turned to face her. "The only bright spot was you. I've so enjoyed our talks. They distracted me from thoughts of her. And yet ... I'm so grateful to you. You took such good care of her. You were with her for so many hours when I couldn't be there."

Diana's hopes faded; he did only feel gratitude. She braved a smile. She couldn't—wouldn't—let her disappointment show.

"I've done a lot of soul-searching," he continued, "and I find I'm no longer content to live with just my memories."

Startled, for a moment all Diana could do was blink. Then he reached for her hand, his warm fingers encircling her own.

"Amanda was an unselfish woman," he said. "She told me she wanted me to go on with my life. She hoped I'd find love again." He squeezed her hand affectionately. "You've been a good friend to me. You let me talk about her—grieve for her. I needed that before I could go on. And now," he paused, and then, "I think I might be in love with you, Diana."

Diana found it hard to speak. For so long she'd hoped he might feel this way, now she was afraid to admit her own feelings. And yet.... "I think I love you, too, Jason."

He glanced around her cozy kitchen and looked embarrassed. "I know this isn't the most romantic setting but, would you be my Valentine?"

Diana was instantly on her feet, drawn into his welcome embrace.

"Oh, Jason. I've waited for this day."

He looked at her with such tenderness. She let her eyes close, waiting, breathless as a teenager anticipating their first kiss. And she was not disappointed. His arms surrounded her and she felt safe . . . wanted.

"Happy Valentine's Day, Diana."

Chapter Six

PRISONER OF LOVE

by Lorraine Bartlett

Whatever were you thinking, Rhonda?" My older sister, Marla, gazed at me with the same stern disapproval I'd too often seen in my own mother's eyes. That look was her legacy and Marla had inherited it.

I didn't have to justify my actions to anyone. All I needed from her was an answer, yes or no. "You're either going to be there for me, or you're not."

Marla frowned and heaved a deep sigh.

"This isn't the way I pictured you getting married. In a prison chapel," she said bitterly.

It wasn't the way I'd visualized my wedding day, either. All my girlhood dreams contained a whitewashed church, stained glass, scented candles, a circlet of flowers in my hair and a white-beaded gown with a twenty-foot train.

Those dreams were now tarnished. I was no longer in my twenties. The man of my dreams hadn't ridden up on a white horse, promising me a life of love, happiness, and security.

Loneliness had driven me to the personals section of our local newspaper. At thirty-five, my biological clock had been ticking loudly. Never one to make the bar scene, and working in an office full of women, made it hard for me to meet men. I'd taken classes, gone on singles trips, but every man I met only seemed interested in a quick roll in the hay. I wanted a lifetime commitment, a home and a family.

The ad I answered gave no real clue of the man who'd written it:

White, single male, non-smoker, loves poetry, quiet walks, sunshine and fresh air. Seeks loving companion. Grow old with me.

I was too embarrassed to tell Marla or anyone else how low desperation had taken me.

The first letter arrived only days after I'd sent my own.

Dear Rhonda,

Thanks for your warm and funny note. Let me tell you a little about myself. I'm a computer programmer, age 32, who loves swimming and hiking. Like you, I read tons of books and love to discuss them at length. I've written some poetry—which has become kind of a new hobby for me.

Please write back and tell me more about yourself. I think we could become friends. I hope we can become more.

Your new friend,

Dave Sanders

A real letter with neat handwriting was so much more romantic than an e-mail and I was glad I'd chosen the old-fashioned route to communicate. I bought new stationery, a pen with pretty purple ink, and answered his letter. That was the beginning of our relationship.

"Something's fishy," Marla said to me after Dave and I had been corresponding for almost two months. "Why hasn't he asked to meet you?"

"Dave's had several bad relationships in the past. He wants to take things slow."

"He's married," Marla said with conviction.

"No, he's not. I already asked him."

"Why do you write letters? Hasn't he got a computer? You could e-mail each other. Why hasn't he called you?"

"Dave's old fashioned. He says people used to take their time to get to know one another. He doesn't want to make the same kinds of mistakes he's made in the past."

Marla's expression hardened. "What kinds of mistakes?"

I shrugged. Dave hadn't given me any specifics.

Marla glanced at Dave's return address on one of the envelopes.

"How come he only has a P.O. Box?"

"He lives in a small, rural town. They don't have house-to-house delivery."

She shook her head. "Be careful, Rhonda. I don't want to see you hurt."

"I'm not going to get hurt," I assured her.

Dave and I wrote often. How I lived for the postman's delivery! Dave's letters were the high point of my day. Sundays were torture without my daily Dave fix.

Then came the day Dave asked for my picture. I'd already looked through the envelopes of snapshots I'd taken during the past few years, but other people had usually been the subjects as I'd been behind the camera.

What I needed was a glamour shot. Surely, that would entice Dave to finally ask to meet me.

The pictures came out gorgeous. With soft lighting and a professional make-up job, I looked like a million bucks.

I sent Dave a five-by-seven-inch print in a pretty silver frame.

Thanks for the picture, Dave wrote. *You're everything I've dreamed about. I hope you won't be disappointed in mine.*

Inside the envelope was a portion of a snapshot. Obviously, Dave had not been the subject of the photo, and he'd cut it down. Warm brown eyes under a fringe of dark wavy hair looked at me. A sweet, shy smile graced his thin lips.

He was just what I'd pictured.

"I think I'm falling in love with you," I wrote that night. "But my family is giving me a hard time. They think you're misleading me. The P.O. Box—the fact that you don't want to meet me in person...."

I didn't receive a letter back for four days. I've blown it, I thought, each day when I checked that empty mailbox.

On the fifth day, I found the familiar white envelope with the handwriting I'd come to love.

My dearest Rhonda,

Your family is right to be protective of you. I didn't want you to judge me before you got to know me. Now that you've admitted your feelings for me, I hope you are as pleased to learn I feel the same way about you.

Unfortunately, I'm not in a position to come see you. I do live in a rural town—in Mastin, at the Correctional Facility.

"I knew it. He's a jailbird!" Marla wailed when I told her.

"Dave was wrongfully convicted," I said.

"Oh, Rhonda," she said, tears welling in her eyes. "Don't tell me you believe him?"

"Of course I do."

Marla shook her head sadly. "What crime?"

I turned away from her. "That's not important."

"It most certainly is. Tell me."

I couldn't look my sister in the eye. "Rape."

"Oh, Rhonda, no! Please don't say you've fallen for a man who could do that to a woman!"

I whirled to confront her. "Dave is innocent."

"How do you know?"

I didn't. And I'd already thought of every argument she might have come up with to discourage me from continuing my relationship with Dave.

"How long has he been in jail, anyway?" Marla asked.

"Nine years. He'll be eligible for parole next fall. He's been a model prisoner. He's even earned a college degree in computer science. He's—"

Marla held up her hand to stop me. "Don't say anymore. I can tell by the set of your chin that you've already made up your mind about this loser."

"Dave's not a loser," I said hotly.

"Have it your way," Marla said. "Just be careful."

Marla left my apartment, giving me too much to think about.

I loved my sister, my only remaining immediate family member. I loved Dave. If we were ever to have a chance at a life together, I had to look into Dave's eyes to see for myself if he could indeed have committed such a heinous crime.

The Mastin Correctional Facility was a medium security prison located an hour from my hometown. Razor wire on high fences kept prisoners inside its brick walls. I arrived at the visitor center bright and early one Saturday, in the company of other women, some of whom had brought their children.

Female guards searched me for contraband, and my purse was emptied, but I was soon ushered into the meeting room. I'd thought the prisoners would be behind a plastic barrier, and despite my excitement at meeting the man with whom I'd shared so many of my dreams, I felt nervous to be so close to him.

I knew Dave the moment I saw him. The drab, prison-issue coveralls couldn't hide his lean, well-muscled body. My knees went rubbery as he clasped my hands and looked into my eyes.

"Thank you for coming, Rhonda. I was so afraid that knowing about my past would color your feelings against me."

We talked about nonsensical things for most of my first visit: the weather, our favorite foods. Near the end of the hour, I forced myself to ask the dreaded question.

"Did you rape that woman?"

Dave's eyes filled and his lips pursed. "I swear, on my mother's life, I could never have done what they convicted me for."

"Then how—why?"

"I lived on the same street as the woman who said I raped her. I didn't know her—had never met her. All I can figure is I must have looked like the man who hurt her. I swear to you, Rhonda, I didn't do it!"

"All men behind bars are innocent," Marla said snidely when I told her about my visit.

"I believe Dave," I said, "with all my heart."

Marla scowled. "Why didn't he appeal his case?"

"He couldn't afford it. He...."

Marla shook her head. "You poor, misguided girl. You always were a sucker for a sob story."

Anger surged through me. "That's a lie!"

"Then how about the lemon of a car you bought from Tim Maxwell? You wouldn't even take him to small claims court."

"How could I? His mother was dying of cancer."

"I saw her in the grocery store yesterday. She looked fine."

"You know experimental drugs saved her life."

"Yes, but it was her health insurance, not the two grand Tim bilked from you, that paid for it."

I wasn't about to argue with her.

"I won't listen to you talk bad about Dave. You don't know him like I do."

"I hope to never know him. Look how he misrepresented himself. Letting you fall in love with him before he told you the truth about his past. Rhonda, dear little sister, Dave's using you!"

"What for?"

"That's a good question. One you should be asking him!"

I watched Marla's car pull away and knew if I was ever to have a lasting relationship with Dave, I'd have to prove to Marla what Dave's court-appointed attorney had not been able to prove to a jury: that Dave had been wrongly convicted.

My first step was to unearth the newspaper reports on the crime. The public library's microfilmed records provided those. Dave had been arrested in January ten years before. I found the account on the Police Blotter. It said simply: David M. Sanders, 22, of 67 Marlborough Street, was arrested for rape.

His trial, in city court, lasted two days. The unnamed woman (they protected her name, but not Dave's), testified that a man matching Dave's description had broken into her apartment and raped her at knifepoint.

As I read through the account, it occurred to me that the evidence presented was pretty circumstantial. Dave had been home alone at the time of the crime, with no one to verify his alibi. Although he'd never so much as had a parking ticket, the judge had given him a sentence of fifteen years.

I thought about what I'd read and I realized there'd been no mention of DNA evidence. I knew that ten years ago they used blood tests to clear or convict suspects. Was it possible to have the evidence rechecked using the new technology? If Dave was innocent, and I believed he was, that would be the only way to clear him.

I wrote Dave immediately and told him I'd be up to see him on the next visiting day to discuss the matter further.

In the meantime, I went on the Internet and tried to find out if such testing could be authorized. Did I need a judge's order? Would I need an attorney? What were the laws in our state for reopening old cases?

Armed with new knowledge, I headed for the prison to see Dave.

Instead of being happy with me, Dave's face bore a frown.

"Don't push this, Rhonda. I'm due for parole in a few months. I want out of here so bad—"

"But, Dave, you're a convicted felon. If we can't clear your name, you'll carry that stigma with you the rest of your life!"

Dave's eyes were grave. "Don't stir up trouble for me, Rhonda."

"He's guilty," Marla told me the next day. "Otherwise he'd be begging you to help him."

I admit that Dave's refusal to have the evidence DNA tested had shaken my faith in him—if only just a little. Yet I couldn't believe the man who had written such tender love poetry could ever treat a woman with the violence he'd been convicted of.

Despite Dave's objections, I decided to pursue the matter.

Luck was with me. About the same time, the State decided to review old prosecution evidence in felony crimes. I hired a high-priced lawyer from the biggest firm in town, Benson, Johns, and Stanhope.

Jared Stanhope's kind blue eyes looked at me over his half-glasses, studying my face. I immediately liked him upon shaking hands. His were smooth, warm and dry, his handshake firm but not crushing. The silver at his temples contrasted nicely with the rest of his thick, dark hair. An aura of confidence surrounded him, and I knew I'd be able to trust him with my life. With Dave's future....

"You know, Miss Roberts, that this will be difficult without Mr. Saunders' full cooperation."

"Yes," I said.

"First we'll have to determine if the evidence still exists."

"You mean it might have been destroyed?"

"It's a real possibility. Also, some prosecutors have resisted allowing old evidence to be tested. It upsets their conviction rate for old crimes to be overturned."

"You don't give me much hope," I said.

"I want you to be aware of the difficulties we might encounter. I know several people in the DA's office. Lucky for us, this isn't an election year. I'll see what I can do."

I didn't mention any of that in my letters to Dave. His letters didn't come quite so often, and there was a chilly standoffishness to them that stung me.

Couldn't he see I only wanted what was best for him? Couldn't he see how clearing his name would make his life better?

He's guilty, said an insidious little voice inside my head. That's why he's against this. He raped that woman and is playing you for a fool.

I didn't want to believe it. Didn't want to believe that I could fall for a man who could attack and threaten a woman, forever taking away her sense of security; stealing her dignity.

Instead, I concentrated on the bright future I'd have with Dave. How we'd marry, have children, and build a new life together.

Jared Stanhope kept me up to date on the progress he was making on the case, and I struggled to work all the overtime I could get to pay his fees. I began to look forward to his weekly calls, surprised at how personable he was. Not at all what I would have expected from someone in his position.

It was weeks before we learned the evidence against Dave had not been destroyed and, after some persuasion from Jared, Dave had consented to give a DNA sample to the County Prosecutor's office.

I had hoped Dave's letters would have been more upbeat. Giving the sample had to prove Marla wrong. Dave was actively cooperating. He'd have never let himself be tested if there was any chance he'd be proven guilty.

We didn't discuss the case in our letters, or at my monthly visits to the prison.

Dave seemed different, restless. I wasn't sure how to cheer him, except with talk of the future.

I wasn't always sure he was listening to me. Often he had a faraway look in his eyes. But when he'd smile, I took comfort that everything would be all right.

"Once Dave's found innocent, we won't have to get married in the prison chapel," I told Marla. "I'll contact a justice of the peace and we can exchange our vows at a pavilion in the park. It'll be a simple but lovely wedding. You'll see."

Marla didn't comment.

I had to believe in the future—in my future with Dave. That we'd be married as soon as he was released.

I bought a tea-length gown of ivory satin, selected a florist and a caterer. All I needed now was the groom and the wedding date.

We waited two long months for the wheels of justice to turn.

It was a rainy Tuesday evening, and I'd just walked in the door when the phone rang. I ran to catch it before the answering machine would get it.

"Hello?"

"Rhonda, it's Jared."

My stomach tightened. He'd never called so late.

"Good news or bad?" I asked with trepidation.

"That depends on your point of view."

My hand tightened on the receiver, and a puddle began to form around my already soggy shoes. "Hit me with the bad news first."

"We probably won't be chatting on the phone much in the future. Too bad. I've so enjoyed our conversations."

I frowned. "I don't understand."

"Dave's tests came back negative, proving he couldn't have raped that woman."

A wave of giddiness passed through me. I fell into one of my kitchen chairs. "Thank God," I breathed. "When—when will they release him?"

"If we're lucky, within the week. I'll keep you posted."

"Oh, Jared, thank you. I'm so happy I could kiss you."

"I'm so happy I would let you," he said.

Jared and I spoke often during the next few days; we even met for lunch so that I could inspect the paperwork that would set Dave free.

He reached for my hand over coffee. "You're a remarkable woman, Rhonda. You have a lot of love to give. I just hope you'll be happy. That you truly know...." His words trailed off and he turned his gaze to our clasped fingers.

I studied Jared's face, noticing the fine lines etched around his eyes, and the sadness in them. Why did I have to meet him now, when I was so in love in Dave? Jared possessed everything I'd always wanted in a man: strength, integrity, and most of all kindness.

If things had been only different....

I pulled my hand back, feeling disloyal to Dave.

"You've been a good friend, Jared. Dave and I will always be grateful to you."

Jared's lips pursed. He looked like he wanted to say something more, but the waitress approached the table and set the check before him.

I gathered up my purse. "I'll see you in court," I said and fled the restaurant.

Three days later, Dave and Jared stood before the judge. I sat behind the defense table, beaming with pride in my soon-to-be husband, and happy to be able to tell Marla "I told you so."

The judge called Dave to stand before his bench.

"It is with great regret that this court must agree that you were wrongfully convicted and imprisoned for the crime of rape. You are hereby set free."

There were papers to sign before the judge finally banged his gavel.

Dave turned to Jared. "Thanks, Mr. Stanhope. I don't know what else to say." He offered his hand and they shook.

Jared glanced at me. "You can thank Miss Roberts. It was her faith in you that persuaded me to take the case."

Dave's smile was wistful. "Thank you, Rhonda."

I moved to stand beside the man I loved, giving him a quick kiss. Dave seemed embarrassed, and my love for him swelled.

"Call me in a day or so," Jared told Dave. "Next we go after the State for damages. They owe you nine years of your life. Or at least the financial equivalent."

The court continued to empty and I clasped Dave's sweating hand.

"This means a new beginning for us," I said.

Dave hung his head, his smile fading. "I'm afraid it doesn't, Rhonda."

"Honey?" came a voice from the open doorway.

Dave's head snapped up, his eyes alight with pure joy.

A petite blonde, in her early twenties, dressed in a dark blue tailored suit, with matching pumps and purse, stood framed in the doorway before us. Dave rushed to her side, kissed her mouth, and they embraced.

"Sorry I'm late," she said breathlessly.

"You're here now," he said and smiled at her.

For a moment, I just stood there, too dumbfounded to speak, groping for a possible explanation. His sister? A very affectionate cousin?

Dave pulled back, clasped her hand and led her forward.

"Rhonda, I want you to meet Sue Abrams. My fiancée."

"Your...fian—" I choked on the word.

How could this be? How could—?

"But, you and I. I thought...."

"You've been a wonderful friend, Rhonda. The best. Without you, Sue and I wouldn't have a chance at a future together."

"Wait a minute," I cried. "What about all those letters? What about all those visits to the prison? Didn't you understand how I felt about you, how I—"

"I tried to let you down gently," Dave said, looking at Sue for support. "If you remember, I never talked about a future together. You were...my pen pal. I'm afraid that's all you ever were."

He couldn't have hurt me more if he'd slapped me.

"But after I told you I loved you, you said you shared those feelings."

"I do love you. As a friend."

"But the love poetry.... I thought you were writing about me —about us!"

Dave shook his head. "I'm sorry, Rhonda. I truly am."

I didn't know what to say—couldn't utter a word.

"Jared thinks I'll get a big settlement from the State," Dave continued. "I'll repay you for all the legal fees. It's the least I can do."

The least he could do? I still couldn't speak.

"We'd better go," Sue said, looking embarrassed. "Thank you, Miss Roberts, for all you've done for Dave."

Tears were streaming down my cheeks.

Dave's mouth moved, but no words came out. Then, still clasping Sue's hand, he turned and led her from the empty courtroom.

I sank into one of the hard wooden chairs. How could I have been such a sap? How many other women had Dave been writing to? Had they all fallen for his golden words like I had?

Dave wasn't a rapist, but he was a heel.

But if I was honest with myself, I should've seen how in recent months how his attitude toward me had changed. His manner, in his letters and during our visits, had become restrained. I'd taken it as a sign he was worried about the ruling. Instead, he'd been corresponding—falling in love—with Sue. She was younger and prettier than me.

I'd spent thousands of dollars to free the man from jail, and all I had to show for it was a stack of canceled checks.

I bowed my head, the tears coming faster now, the sounds of my sobs echoing in that cavernous room.

Suddenly a hand thrust a handkerchief before my swimming eyes. I looked up to see Jared Stanhope standing over me, his patient face filled with compassion.

"You knew?" I asked.

He nodded solemnly. "I suspected for some time. Dave only told me yesterday. I'm sorry, Rhonda."

I wiped my eyes and blew my nose. Jared sat down beside me.

"It's not the end of the world, you know," he said.

"Oh, no? I look like a fool. I look like—"

"A woman of great compassion, who'd go to the ends of the

earth to see that justice prevailed," he finished for me. "Don't take what you've done lightly. You proved Dave was innocent, got him released from jail. That was no easy feat."

"I've been stupid. What will my friends—my sister—think when they find out about this?"

"You only have to live with yourself. And I'd say you should feel proud."

I dabbed at my eyes. I didn't feel proud. I felt like a jerk.

"I know it's early," Jared said, "but I wonder if you'd be interested in having dinner with me?"

I looked into those kind blue eyes. He was just being nice. But right then, I needed someone to be nice to me. I needed someone's compassion. I needed a friend.

"You don't have to—" I started to protest.

Jared touched my lips with his finger to stop me. A quiver of excitement went through me.

"Maybe Dave only looked at you as a friend, but I'd like to get to know you on a more personal basis. That is if you wouldn't mind."

I blinked at Jared's sincere face. "Really?"

His smile was sincere. "Really." He rose from the chair and offered me his hand.

I took it, and we walked out of the courtroom together.

~

Chapter Seven

BLUE CHRISTMAS

by Lorraine Bartlett

"Hey, Judi, got any plans for the holiday?"

Judi Straub closed her eyes and silently counted to ten. If there was one question she absolutely loathed it was about her holiday plans, and yet, it seemed as if everyone in her office had asked her that question in the days preceding Thanksgiving. They all knew she was single, with no prospects, and not much in the way of immediate family, either.

"Nothing special. Just going to watch the Macy's parade on TV, and then sit down and read a good book."

"Alone?" Carol asked.

Judi nodded.

"Oh, but you can't do that. We've got plenty of room at my house. Why don't you bring a dish to pass and join us? I know Larry would love it, and so would the kids."

That was laying it on a bit thick. While Judi had met Carol's husband at work affairs, she'd never met their kids. The ones Carol complained about on a regular basis. The hooligans, she called them, since it always seemed like they were in trouble at school or at home.

"That's very sweet, but I don't want to impose."

"It's not an imposition. Larry already invited one of his pals from work. Maybe the two of you could get together."

Oh, no! First a dinner invitation, now Carol was trying to fix her up with yet another dud. *No, thanks.* But Carol had been right, she absolutely refused to take no for an answer.

And so on Thanksgiving day, Judi found herself standing in Carol's kitchen, chopping vegetables, sautéing onions for the stuffing, and washing far too many pots and pans.

If that wasn't bad enough, when Larry's newly divorced friend, Ed, showed up, he was just a little drunk. Carol immediately pushed Judi on him and all the man could talk about was his ex-wife, their children, whom she'd turned against him, and how worried he was about getting fired because—surprise!—he'd been drinking too much.

When they all sat down for dinner, Judi found she was stuck in front of a table leg with no elbow room. For some reason, Carol's parents weren't speaking to each other, but glared at each other across the table, and the hooligans did nothing but bicker. The dishes weren't anything like Judi was used to eating, either. Canned corn, green bean casserole, and turkey so dry the taste and texture resembled cardboard. And the ultimate sacrilege: the gravy came straight out of a jar.

Of course, Carol worked a full-time job. She didn't have time to prepare an elaborate meal from scratch, but the only dish Judi found even halfway palatable was the homemade cranberry sauce she'd made herself. However, no one else at the table touched it, preferring the jellied kind that not only came from a can but retained that shape until it was attacked by the hungry mob.

Ed continued to drink during the meal, and when dessert was served, he brought down the house by vomiting all over the chocolate cream pie. The hooligans laughed with delight, while Carol's parents got up from the table and left the house in a hurry.

With bad grace, Carol cleaned up that mess and then asked

Larry to drive his friend home. Judi would have liked to have taken off, too, but got roped into helping Carol with the dishes and washing yet more pots.

Never again, she vowed.

Of course, in years past, Thanksgiving had been a lot of fun, before Judi's parents' health declined. Her mother would host the dinner with chestnut stuffing, a turkey so big it barely fit the oven, yams, whipped potatoes, luscious homemade gravy, at least three pies, as well as cookies, and a cake. There was always too much food and everyone waddled as they'd left the table. Judi, her sister Pam and her family, made it every year, and her brother Bill and his family would alternate the holidays with his wife's family.

At forty and the youngest, Judi had never married, although she'd been engaged twice. She lived with her parents and took on more and more responsibility for the house as they declined. It hurt when she found out either Pam or Bill would throw a holiday party and not invite her. "You know Mom and Dad couldn't navigate to come to our house—not with all those stairs," Pam explained. "They'd be hurt if I invited you and not them." Apparently, it hadn't occurred to Pam that Judi's feelings might be hurt to be excluded from the festivities.

Still, what would the holidays be if they weren't spent with her parents? So even though her mother hadn't been able to do much of the work anymore, Judi worked hard to provide the kind of Thanksgiving her family had always known, even taking days of vacation leading up to the holiday to complete the cleaning and cooking. Somehow, at the end of the meal, she was up to her elbows in dishwater scrubbing the pots and pans while everyone else gathered around the TV to watch football.

But even that tradition changed when some three years later their mother died from a massive heart attack. Their father never recovered from the loss and followed her in death from a stroke less than a year later.

Pam made a huge production of hosting Christmas that first year without their parents, but then Bill's wife started a fight over the lack of cloth napkins and vowed to never darken Pam's door again. Bill apologized profusely, but he seldom saw his sisters after that disastrous December 25th.

It was a week before Christmas when Judi got a call from Pam. "What are you doing for the holidays?"

Judi cringed but tried to sound ambivalent. "I haven't decided," she said, which was true. She hadn't given it much thought.

"We're going skiing in Vail. Would you like to join us?"

Judi's mouth fell open in surprise. "Oh, Pam. That is so sweet of you to include me."

"Hold on a minute, you can join us—but you'll have to pay your own way."

Judi's joy immediately evaporated. "How much is it liable to cost?"

"It's a lovely upscale resort. You'd want your own room, of course, and it's three hundred forty a night. Plus your airfare. At this late date, you'd probably have to pay a grand or more."

"How long will you be staying?

"Seven days and six nights."

Where did Pam think she'd come up with that kind of money on such short notice? Yes, she had her full one-third share of her parents' estate, but she was determined to save it for retirement.

"And what will you and Brad be doing when you're not on the slopes?"

"Brad's boss will be there, along with his wife, Jean. Brad will work and I'll keep Jean from getting lonely."

"And what about me?"

"I was hoping you could hang out with the kids. Take them skiing and to other lessons. They've got an Olympic size skating rink. You used to love to skate."

Yes, she had—until she'd broken an ankle.

"I'm sorry, Pam. Much as I'd love to go, I don't think I could get the time off from work on such notice."

"Oh, damn. I hadn't thought of that."

"How long have you been planning this trip?"

"About three months."

And she'd only just then remembered that she had three children and no one to dump them on?

"I'm really sorry."

"Don't worry about it. But I hate the thought of you sitting alone on Christmas day."

"It's okay; I've already had a number of invitations from friends and co-workers." All of which she'd turned down.

"Bill wants us to have lunch with him on Wednesday. Do you think you could make it?"

"Bill called you?"

"Yeah, he said he thought it would be the only time he could squeeze us in."

"Magnanimous of him," Judi said, hoping Pam caught the sarcasm in her voice.

"We're meeting at the Gatekeeper restaurant. Do you know where it is?"

"Yes, right next to Bill's office." Of course, he couldn't have chosen a place where Judi wouldn't have to drive half an hour to get there. She'd have to take a couple of hours off from work to be able to make it.

"Sure," she answered. "I'd love to see you both. What time?"

"Noon."

"Okay, I'll see you there."

"Great. Bye."

Judi replaced her phone and looked around the small cubicle she called her home away from home. She'd decorated it with colored lights, set out a bowl of holiday M&Ms, and had her radio tuned into the local soft rock station that had played holiday music 24/7 since before Thanksgiving.

She was about to turn back to her computer when Carol stuck her head inside the door. "Hey, Judi, are you going to participate in the Secret Santa game this year?"

Judi sighed. The year before, she'd been the lucky recipient of a Chia pet. Why on God's earth would an adult buy such an item? She'd given it to her neighbor's daughter, only to hear the girl had broken the ceramic pig before the seeds had had time to germinate.

"Sure, why not," she said, even managing a faint smile.

"Great, the party is on Thursday afternoon."

"Which means I'd better go shopping tonight or tomorrow."

But Carol had already moved on to the next cubicle without listening to Judi's reply.

Much as she hated holiday shopping, later that night Judi found herself wandering the local mall. If she wasn't going to spend the holidays with Pam or Bill, that meant she might be able to get away with just buying each of them a Christmas gift, instead of a separate present for their kids and spouses, too. She found a beautiful cashmere scarf on sale for fifty percent off for Pam, and then visited the liquor store across the street to buy Bill a bottle of expensive single malt scotch, as well as a bottle of red wine for the Secret Santa.

With her shopping complete, Judi headed for home.

Christmas was less than a week away, and though she'd sent her Christmas cards out nearly a week before, she'd yet to receive any. She opened her mailbox to find circulars, credit card applications, and not one Christmas card.

"Bah, humbug," she groused and trudged up the stairs to her second-floor apartment. She'd tried to make the place cheerful by buying a tabletop artificial tree and decorating it with some of the ornaments that had gone on her parents' tree. None of them were favorites; Pam had beaten her to the decorations, along with most of their mother's other treasures. Instead, Judi bought a few colored balls and lights and figured as no one would see the tree except for herself, it would do. She put a Christmas CD on her stereo and wrapped the three gifts, setting them under her tree. They sure looked lonely.

Bill was terribly fond of homemade Christmas cutout cookies, and with two kids he seldom got to eat more than one or two before they were scarfed up. So she measured the ingredients and made the dough, deciding to let it sit in the fridge overnight. She figured she could bake and frost the cookies the next evening and surprise Bill. But it wouldn't do to make cookies for Bill and not have any for Pam, so she doubled the recipe.

Wednesday morning Judi awoke to find it had snowed at least six inches overnight. The plow had already visited her apartment's parking lot, blocking her in. Opening the trunk of her car, she withdrew the shovel she kept for just such an occurrence and dug her way out. Traffic was as slow as molasses, so of course she showed up almost an hour late for work, which she was allowed to take as vacation time. The Christmas spirit was certainly scarce at Rogers and Meriwether Incorporated.

All too soon it was eleven-thirty, and Judi grabbed her coat to make her lunch date when a voice stopped her.

"Judi, have you got a minute?" her boss, Ted Andrews, asked.

"A minute is all. I've got a lunch meeting," she said.

"We're expecting the Barnett contract to come in tonight. Can you stay late to help us go over it?

Judi wanted to say no, to scream it, to refuse in no uncertain terms, but instead, she said, "I stayed the last two times a contract came in late. Can't Carol handle it?"

Ted laughed. "Come on, Judi, you know Carol has a family."

"And what's that got to do with it?"

"It's Christmastime."

"I don't see your point."

"Well, you haven't got anything better to do."

"How do you know?"

"You're single. And if office gossip is correct, you haven't even had a date in over three years."

Judi felt her cheeks grow hot in embarrassment, but she forced herself not to speak her mind.

"Tell you what. I'll sweeten the deal. We're letting everyone go an hour early on Friday. If you work tonight, on Friday you can leave at three instead of four o'clock."

Big Hairy Deal! Judi wanted to scream, but instead, she said. "Okay. I've got to go."

"Have a nice lunch!" Ted called after her.

The roads were in better shape than they'd been during the morning rush hour, but were still slippery in spots. Cleveland looked a whole lot better covered in snow than it did the rest of the time, but it wasn't beauty she craved at that moment—just some peace and quiet and an uneventful drive across town.

She was ten minutes late when she finally made it to the restaurant carrying her purse, and a large shopping bag containing the scarf, the bottle, and the Tupperware containers filled with cookies. Pam and Bill were already seated at the table and had ordered a round of drinks—for themselves.

"Merry Christmas," Judi called and bent down to give each of her siblings a kiss.

"Hey, little sister. Great to see you," Bill said. "And what have you got there?"

"Just a couple of gifts for the two of you."

"Oh, dear," Pam said, sounding embarrassed. "I'm afraid I didn't get anything for you."

"Me, either," Bill said.

Again, Judi felt her cheeks redden. "That's okay. It's no big deal," she said and passed around the gifts and the containers of cookies.

"Hey, my favorite," Bill said after unwrapping the scotch.

"Oh, this scarf is lovely," Pam said. It'll go perfectly with the coat Brad's giving me for Christmas."

"How do you know he's giving you a coat?" Judi asked.

Pam giggled. "I peeked."

"Thanks for the cookies. We have a party to go to tonight. We're supposed to bring something—this will be great."

"But I made them just for you. I didn't want you to have to share."

"That's okay. It'll save Jean from fussing. You know how she gets."

Judi and Pam shared a knowing look; they sure did.

The waiter arrived and asked for their orders. Since they'd neglected to tell him they had a third person joining them, there was no menu at Judi's spot. Bill ordered for himself and passed his along to Judi. She glanced at it, but all too soon the waiter turned to her for her order. "I'll have the chef's salad with ranch dressing on the side."

"Very good, madam," said the waiter, and took the menu from her.

Bill had ordered the seared tuna, and Pam had ordered lobster —two of the most expensive items on the menu. "What the heck," Pam had said. "It's Christmastime." She and Bill had a ordered a second round of drinks, but knowing she had to work late, Judi passed on ordering a glass of wine for herself.

All too soon, lunch was over and the check arrived. "Why don't we just make it easy on ourselves and split it three ways," Bill said.

"That sounds reasonable to me," Pam agreed.

"Wait a minute. I didn't have any drinks. And I only ordered a small salad."

"Come on, Judi. It's Christmas. Don't be such a skinflint," Pam said with a laugh.

Judi fought tears as she dug into her wallet to come up with her one-third share. She and Pam handed money to Bill, who promptly took out his credit card. "Since I told you a little about what I'm working on, I can put this on my expense account."

"But that's dishonest, Bill," Judi pointed out.

"Get a life, kid," he said, handing the waiter the leather folder with the check.

Judi looked at her watch. "I have to get going." She shrugged into the sleeves of her coat, but this time didn't offer her brother and sister a kiss. "Merry Christmas," she said, and for the first time in her life did not mean the sentiment.

"Have a good Christmas," Bill called to her back. Judi didn't hear if Pam wished her a happy holiday.

Judi got in her car, put the key in the ignition, and sat there for a long moment fighting tears. Who were those people she'd just spent ninety minutes with? They weren't the siblings she'd known years ago. Bill had been her protector from the bullies at school. Pam had shared her lipsticks and given her tips on how to fix her hair and choose clothes. Now they were strangers who had their own lives to live and no time to share with her.

"Never again," she declared. "Never again."

The Barnett contract showed up much later than anyone antici-pated. Judi kept busy, trying to clear off the work that had accu-mulated on her desk while she'd been out for lunch. She was yawning by the time the contract showed up by courier at nine o'clock, and her stomach growled with hunger. She'd assumed that

Ted would order in some food for her and the other three people who'd been coerced into staying late, but while Ted had gone out for a bite, he hadn't brought back a thing for his employees. Vending machine coffee and stale granola bars made a poor substitute for an evening meal.

Judi finally staggered into her apartment at midnight. By then she was so tired, she could barely keep her eyes open long enough to undress and climb under the covers, and neglected to set her alarm for the next morning.

It was already light when she awoke, just forty-five minutes before she was expected at work. One quick shower later, she snatched her grab-bag gift and ran down the stairs and out of the building to her car with her hair still dripping. Luckily, it hadn't snowed overnight, so she jumped right in her car and headed straight for work.

There was no way she could sneak in without being seen; all workers had to swipe their identification cards to enter the building, so Ted would know exactly what time she'd arrived.

No sooner had she hung up her coat, when Ted arrived at the opening to her cubicle. "You're late," he said.

"And after the hours I put in for you yesterday—without pay, I might add—I should think you could cut me some slack."

"I'm only kidding," Ted said, but she could tell that he wasn't. "Don't let it happen again."

Judi fumed in silence.

The morning passed quickly, and all too soon, Carol stuck her head over the cubicle's wall. "Time for the company Christmas party!" she called brightly. "Are you coming?"

"Yes. Just give me a minute to finish this."

"Okay, but you don't want to miss the food for the secret Santa."

"Yeah, I sure don't want that to happen," Judi said without enthusiasm.

The company Christmas party was always the same. Management ordered cold cuts, several cold salads, a tray of cookies, and bottles of soda for the staff. Of course, they always seemed to underestimate the number of employees who were to show up. As Carol had predicted, most of the rolls and cold cuts had disappeared, leaving a few slices of cheese and half a bowl of coleslaw. *Bah, humbug*, Judi groused to herself.

She was about to leave the conference room when Carol tugged at her sleeve. "Did you bring your Secret Santa gift?"

"Yes. It's already up there with the others."

"Aren't you going to wait to see what you get?"

"Last year's gift was so exciting, I'm worried I might faint in anticipation."

"Come on, Judi, don't be such a spoilsport. I saved you a couple of cookies." She handed Judi a napkin wrapped package.

Judi opened it to find two cutout cookies. She took a bite from the top of a Christmas tree. Not as good as those she'd made for Bill and Pam, but not bad, either. "Thanks, Carol."

"Now come on over and sit with me. This will be fun. You'll see."

Yeah. Fun.

They grabbed a couple of seats along the side of the conference room. The table was cleared of food, soiled napkins, dirty paper plates and cups, and the wrapped Secret Santa gifts were moved to take their place. Everyone reached into a hat and pulled out a number.

"The rules of the game are this: I'll call a number and you'll take your gift from the pile. But you can't open it. Once everyone has their gift, we'll collect the numbers and everyone will take another one from the hat. They can either keep their gift or take one from someone else. We'll have three rounds. Everybody got that?"

"Yes, Ted," they all called out. Only Carol seemed to be particularly enthused about the game. Since the dollar amount of each gift was not to exceed a ten-dollar maximum, there wasn't much to get excited about.

When Judi's number was called, she was chagrined to find she'd received her own gift, which was certainly better than winning a Chia pet.

Soon all the numbers had been called. "And now the real fun begins," Ted said.

The numbers were turned in and everyone got a different one. Surprisingly, Judi's bottle of wine was the most coveted gift. It was swapped back and forth during that second round, and by the time the third round had begun, it was the most sought-after gift.

"Last call," Ted hollered over the boisterous chatter. "Number fourteen."

Mike Fellows grabbed the pretty box—what Judi assumed to be filled with chocolates—and handed her an envelope. *Great,* she thought with ill humor, a ten-dollar gift certificate. She hoped it would at least be redeemable at the grocery store or gas station.

"Okay, everyone," Ted called, "Open your gifts."

Carol ripped the paper off her gift and groaned. "Oh, no. The Chia pet!"

"Hey, you thought it was a terrific gift when I got one last year," Judi reminded her.

"At least I can re-gift it to one of the hooligans for Christmas. Open yours."

"It's just a card and a gift certificate. No big deal."

"Come on, don't be such a spoilsport."

That made twice in one hour that Carol had accused Judi of being a spoilsport. It was becoming annoying.

"Oh, all right." Judi slipped her finger under the end flap, ripping the envelope. She pulled out the card, which had a blue Christmas tree on the front. *How apropos,* she thought. She was sure to have a blue Christmas. A gift card fell from the card, landing on her lap. She opened the wrapping, read the card, and gasped.

"What is it," Carol demanded.

"It's—it's—"

"Who got the all-expenses-paid trip to Puerto Rico?" Ted asked.

"Judi got it—Judi got it!" Carol screamed hysterically. She couldn't have been more excited if she'd won the prize herself.

"Good for you, Judi. There's just one catch. You have to redeem the trip before the end of the year."

"I—I—" Judi stammered.

"Don't worry about taking vacation without scheduling it months in advance. Carol can take on your work while you're gone."

"Hey," Carol protested, but Judi wasn't listening. She was still in shock at winning such a wonderful prize. Meanwhile, all Judi's colleagues glared at her, especially the ones who had passed on the envelope for something they figured had greater value.

"Is it a trip for two?" Carol demanded. "You could take me with you."

"Would you really want to leave Larry and the hooligans at Christmastime?"

"In a heartbeat," Carol said, but then reality seemed to sink in. "They'd hate me if I did."

Ted clapped his hands. "Back to work everyone."

Those already on their feet shuffled through the conference room door, heading for their cubicles. Carol grabbed the last cookie from the tray and followed the rest.

Judi looked up to see Ted towering above her. "I'm glad you won, Judi. I know I come off like a beast at times, but that's my job—to keep everyone working hard and motivated. You're our hardest worker and never complain."

Judi said nothing, wishing they would have rewarded her with a raise, not just an impractical trip. "I don't know what to say."

"Get on the phone to our travel department and have Irma get you on a flight after Christmas."

"Do I have to wait that long?"

"You want to be in Puerto Rico on Christmas Day?" Ted asked, sounding confused.

"Why not? I was only going to spend the day alone at home, anyway."

"That's even better since we'll be shut down for a few days for the holiday. It's a win-win situation."

Judi looked down at the gift card and allowed herself a smile. Being in Puerto Rico alone had to be better than being snubbed by her own family.

"Thanks, Ted. I think I'll talk to Irma now."

It can't be real, Judi said to herself as she headed for Irma's office. She took care of the travel arrangements whenever any of the lawyers required a flight out of Cleveland, or even when they were traveling for non-work destinations, which seemed to happen all too often. Of course, Irma hadn't been at the Christmas party. No one from the upper floors mixed with the worker bees below.

Irma sat at her desk with a spreadsheet plastered across her twenty-seven-inch monitor. She looked up. "Can I help you?" she asked politely, but rather coldly.

Irma was not the most friendly person on staff, but neither was she feared or avoided.

"I've just come from the Christmas party."

"You won the trip to Puerto Rico?"

"Yes. I don't remember anyone ever winning a prize like that in the Secret Santa."

"And you probably won't ever again. Mr. Rogers found he couldn't take the trip after all, and if the tickets weren't used, they wouldn't be refunded."

"That's okay with me," Judi said, trying not to feel like an afterthought. She'd spent most of her life feeling that way. "How can they be used by anyone other than Mr. Rogers?"

"They were bought in the firm's name. You'll have to show your company ID when you get to the airport on Saturday. "

"But Ted said the tickets had to be used by the end of the year."

"They do. And they're for the ten o'clock flight on Saturday morning. Is there a problem with that?"

"Not at all."

"Swing by my office tomorrow before you leave work, and I'll give you the tickets and have the other vouchers ready for you."

"Thanks."

Saturday morning rolled around and Judi drove to the airport in plenty of time to get through security. Carol had offered to drive her, but she'd declined the invitation. Every time she'd spoken to her the previous day, Carol had delivered one nasty zinger after another. Of course, she was jealous, but did she have to take it out on Judi? There was no way she could have used the trip, so why be so snarky?

Judi left her car in the long-term parking lot and headed for the terminal. The whole idea of the trip seemed unreal, and she felt excitement building within her.

The flight was bumpy, and a toddler two rows ahead of her whined or cried the entire way. Judi pushed the earbuds further into her ears and tried to ignore it, fixing her attention on the novel on her e-reader.

When the plane finally landed, Judi was one of the last people off. She walked through the terminal, found her luggage, and stepped outside to hail a cab. The sun beat down on everything, but the breeze was balmy, so unlike Cleveland in December.

The cab driver was a chatterbox, telling Judi all the places she ought to see while on the island. She might ... but more likely she'd sit on the beach and read, read, read for relaxation.

The first disappointment arrived at the hotel. The suite that was referenced on the paperwork Irma had given her had been downgraded to a single room. That was okay, she thought until she got to the room. The window overlooked the high rise next door, and the full-sized mattress was lumpy. *It's free, it's all free*, she kept telling herself. But it wasn't all-expenses paid after all. She'd still have to pay for her food. Unlike the big boss, she wasn't a partner in the firm traveling on business. No deductions for her. Still, she changed into her swimsuit and her coverall and headed for the beach.

The hotel was situated right on the shore with a large pool available for its guests, complete with piles of towels and lounge chairs, all of which seemed to be taken. Judi grabbed a couple of towels and continued on her way.

The white sands of Puerto Rico were certainly inviting and the beach was packed full of sunburned tourists. Children splashed and dodged the waves, squealing with delight. Judi walked down the beach until she found a less popular spot.

She continued reading the delicious romance novel she'd started on the plane, finishing it as the sun began to sink into the ocean. The beach had emptied and she brushed the sand from her legs before heading back to the hotel for dinner. After changing, she headed down to the hotel's restaurant, but the prices were way out of her league. She visited the front desk.

"Are there any modestly priced restaurants within walking distance?"

There weren't.

So, back to the restaurant she went, ordering an appetizer and a glass of water. It would have to do. And what was she going to do for breakfast and lunch on Christmas day? She sat all alone at her table, trying not to feel jealous of the well-dressed women accompanied by handsome men who occupied the nearby tables. It was then she realized she was truly alone on Christmas Eve. If she'd been home, she might have gone to church. If she were home, she might have gone to the movies. If she were home, she'd have gone to visit her parents' graves.

After finishing her dinner, she took out her e-reader and sat in the lobby. A beautiful tree had been erected, covered with tiny white lights and green and gold ribbons, but somehow the sight made her feel lonelier still. Why had she ever agreed to take this vacation alone? She'd never traveled by herself. It was supposed to be an adventure, but adventures, she discovered, were more enjoyable when you had someone to share them with.

Judi slept in on Christmas morning. After all, she had nothing planned. A continental breakfast spread filled the lobby bar, and Judi chose a muffin and coffee and was shocked to pay over $10 for the pleasure. She looked on the bright side: perhaps she'd lose weight while on vacation.

Although the sky was overcast, she donned her bathing suit and passed the pool, already filled with screaming children, and headed for the beach. *Merry Christmas*, she told herself, finding the beach nearly empty. She settled down on the sand, switched on her e-reader only to find the battery was spent. Was that an omen of things to come?

Judi pulled her knees to her chest and fought the urge to cry. Never had she felt so alone. Even the crystal blue water brought her no pleasure.

It must be your own fault you're alone, she berated herself. While taking care of her parents' needs for so long, she'd totally neglected taking care of herself. Most of her friends were married with children and too busy to worry about a forty-year-old single woman. She considered herself attractive, but her dating skills were terribly rusty. Would she even know how to talk to a man? What did that say about her as a person? That she was totally unlovable? So unlovable even her own family would abandon her during the holidays?

Judi picked up a handful of sand and let it trickle through her fingers. Like sands in an hourglass ... her time on the planet was trickling away. She dusted her hands off, hugged her knees and looked out over the ocean once again.

Perhaps she should have bought herself a gift, wrapped it, and opened it on Christmas Day, but that sounded even more pathetic. Perhaps what she should do is make a Christmas wish. It was a game she and Pam had played while waiting for Santa's arrival in the wee hours of Christmas days past.

With nothing else to do, she thought about all the things she could wish for. A vacation trip. Got that. A new wardrobe? Didn't need that. A pay raise? Forget about that. Eventually, she realized she had only one Christmas wish—never to be lonely again.

Judi smiled in spite of herself. It was such a foolish waste of time to wish for things that might never come true. Still, she closed her eyes, tilted her head toward the sky, and felt the warm breeze wash over her, playing with the loose strands of hair around her face.

I wish with all my heart to find my special someone.

It felt good to hear the words in her mind because she knew it would sound absolutely stupid if she said them aloud—even if there was no one nearby to hear them.

When she opened her eyes, she was startled to find a man standing over her. Not terribly tall, not terribly good looking, with graying brown hair and brown eyes. "Oh, hello. Am I disturbing you?"

"No," Judi said, feeling a little foolish. How long had he been there?

"You look a bit ... well, lonely. Would you like some company?"

Judi looked him over. He looked nice enough, but ... it was a lonely beach, and she was on her own, and ... didn't perverts and molesters comb such places just looking for victims?

Before she could answer, he spoke again.

"I'm out looking for sea glass." He reached into his pockets. "See? Pretty aren't they?" His voice held the hint of an English accent.

"Yes, they are. What are you going to do with them?"

He shrugged, putting them back in his pocket. "Probably make a necklace. It's my hobby, you see. I come out to the beach whenever I have a day off and look for sea glass and other interesting stuff. Why don't you come along and look with me? We can walk up the beach, back toward your hotel. Which way is it?"

Judi felt a little uncomfortable admitting where she was staying. She didn't know this guy from a hole in the ground. "That way," she said and pointed.

"Come on," he said and headed back toward the water where the waves were gently lapping against the sand.

For some reason, Judi picked up her beach towel, wrapped it around her waist, and followed him.

"My name's Harry, what's yours?"

"Harry—like the prince?"

He laughed. "That's it exactly, only I don't have a title or a heady inheritance looming in the future."

"I'm no princess, either. But if you wish, you may call me Princess Judi."

"Like Judy Garland?"

"No, like Judi Dench. My mother was a huge fan."

"As am I," Harry said. He bent down to examine a stone, picked it up, inspected it, and tossed it back into the surf.

"Is sea glass very common?" Judi asked, poking the sand with the toe of her flip-flops.

"Not as much as it used to be. Cruise ships don't dump their garbage the way they used to, which is good for the ocean, but not good for finding sea glass. They've really cracked down on littering, which is good for the island. Who wants to live in a dump?"

"So you live here in Puerto Rico?" she asked.

"Three hundred and sixty-five days of the year. Where are you from?"

"Cleveland."

"Of course—the Rock and Roll Hall of Fame."

"You've got it." She bent down, and picked up a shell, examining the delicate ridges and pale iridescent colors. "I'm an administrative assistant for a large legal firm. What do you do?"

"I have my own business."

"Selling handmade jewelry to the tourists?"

Again he laughed. It was a pleasant sound. "No, that's just a hobby of mine. During the week, I'm an accountant. If you need advice about the tax rules, I'm your man."

"And your family?" she asked and resumed walking along the shore.

"I have a brother and sister back in England, but nobody here in the States."

"No wife and kids?"

He shook his head.

"What brought you here to Puerto Rico?" she asked.

"The miserable winter weather in London. How is it you're here all alone on Christmas Day?"

"I won an all-expenses-paid trip, which is turning out not to be an all-expenses-paid trip. I guess I should have known better."

"But you're here now, and you may as well make the most of it."

"You're right. I will."

"No husband and children?" he asked.

"No. It just never happened."

The sun peeked out from behind the clouds. "Looks like it's going to be another fine day," Harry said.

"And hot?"

"If we're lucky. There's shade by those trees, would you like to go sit there?"

Judi looked around. More and more people had brought towels out to the beach. She decided she'd be safe enough sitting and talking with this stranger.

And talk they did—straight through lunch. Harry told her about his life, and she shared the boring details of her own life.

"You're not boring at all," Harry assured her. "You just need to add a little spice to your life. Speaking of spice, I know a great little restaurant that serves the best jerk chicken."

"I thought that was Jamaican cuisine."

"It is, and it's delicious. Will you join me?"

"I'd love to."

Judi spent every day walking the beach with Harry, talking, laughing, and enjoying each other's company. He invited her to his house for dinner on her last night on the island. He'd made Beef Wellington and served gin and tonics. And afterward, they made love for the first time. Harry hadn't pushed her, and in fact was apologetic that he didn't have any condoms, but Judi had visited the hotel gift shop and bought a box before he picked her up in his rust bucket of a car. She wanted her last night in Puerto Rico to be a memory she'd keep in her heart forever.

At midnight, he delivered her back to her hotel. "I'll take you to the airport in the morning."

"Thank you. I'd appreciate that."

They kissed goodnight, a warm passionate kiss that she relived over and over again in her dreams.

All too soon it was morning, and as promised, Harry showed up with his car. He helped Judi load her suitcase in the trunk, and off they went. The trip was silent, with both of them lost in thought, but before he reached the airport, Harry pulled off to the side of the road. "I can't just let you leave like this, Judi."

"Believe me, I don't want to go back to my old life, either."

"Then stay here with me."

"Much as I would like to, I can't. I have family back in Cleveland."

"How often do you see them?"

Judi sighed. "A couple of times a year."

"And what do you do in the evenings when you're alone?"

She frowned. "Read books or watch TV."

"You don't even have a cat to keep you company."

No, she didn't.

"Marry me," Harry blurted.

Judi blinked in astonishment. "No."

"Why not?"

"Because it just wouldn't work out."

"Why wouldn't it? I make a good living. You could find work here; we could spend our evenings and weekends together for the rest of our lives."

"I'm just not a risk taker, and leaving everything I know would be a really big risk." She studied his face. His eyes looked so, so sad. "I'm sure you'll find another lonely woman on the beach."

"But I don't want someone else. I want you." The sincerity in his voice nearly broke her heart. What they'd shared was a week-long fling—nothing more. But oh, how Judi wished it could have been more.

"I wish I could come inside and stay with you until your flight leaves."

"I do, too."

Harry pulled out a wad of tissue paper from his pants pocket. "For you."

"Oh, Harry, you shouldn't have."

"Something to remember me by."

"It's not like we'll never communicate again. I have your e-mail address and you have mine."

"Yes, but this is something tangible."

Judi accepted the small package, unfolded the tissue and found a piece of sea glass threaded through a silver chain. "Oh, Harry. It's beautiful."

"Will you put it on for me? I'd love to see you wear it."

Judi passed the necklace to Harry, who fastened it around her neck. She reached up to touch the pale green glass. "Thank you."

"Don't ever take it off. I want you to remember me and the precious few hours we've been able to spend together."

"I won't."

Harry kissed her, and then shifted the car into drive and started off for the airport once again.

He pulled up to the curb, and they both got out. He took her suitcase from the trunk and handed it to her. "I'm not going to say good-bye. Just ... until we meet again."

He pulled her into a fierce hug that lasted far too long—then they shared just one more passionate kiss before she had to go.

"E-mail me the minute you get in."

"I will," Judi promised.

There was nothing left to do but leave. Judi turned for the terminal doors, tears blurring her vision, and didn't look back.

Monday morning rolled around and Judi found herself loathing the idea of returning to Rogers and Meriwether. She'd spent the day before doing laundry and putting away her suitcase. The only thing that kept her going was knowing she and Harry could share e-mails. But how long would that last? He might go beach-combing that very afternoon and find yet another lonely middle-aged woman.

No sooner had she arrived at her desk when the phone rang. "Judi Straub," she answered automatically.

"Thank God, where have you been?" Pam demanded. "I've been calling you for days."

She hadn't called the evening before.

"I've been on holiday in Puerto Rico," Judi said.

"Holiday? You mean vacation?"

"Yes."

"Well, you might have said you were going. In fact, you told me just before Christmas that you couldn't afford to go skiing with us. Was that a lie?"

"Of course not. I won the grand prize at my company's Secret Santa. A trip to Puerto Rico."

"You could have told me you were leaving the country."

"Puerto Rico is part of the US—no passports required."

"Weren't you terribly lonely?"

"Not at all. In fact, I met someone while I was there." She decided to annoy her sister. "In fact, he asked me to marry him."

"I hope you said no. What was he, some kind of beach bum looking for an American to support him?"

"Actually, he's an accountant."

"What's his name?"

"I don't see how that's relevant."

"Humor me."

"Oh, all right. Harry Powell."

"And *are* you going to marry him?" Pam demanded.

"Of course not. It was a vacation fling."

"You were flinging with him?" Pam asked, appalled.

"I am a grown-up, not that you or Bill have ever acknowledged that."

Pam said nothing for several long moments. "You aren't thinking of going back to him, are you?"

"No. I told you, it was just a fling."

"I can't believe how foolishly you've behaved. You could catch a disease. I'll bet he spends all his free time looking for women to screw."

"He was a nice guy. Now let's drop it. Why did you call?"

"To find out if you're okay. I do worry about you, you know."

Not so I would notice, Judi thought. "Look, I've been away from my desk for over a week. There's a ton of work I need to catch up on. I'll talk to you later."

"You better believe you will," Pam said and hung up.

Judi replaced the receiver and reached up to touch the piece of sea glass that hung around her neck. How she wished that what she and Harry had shared could be considered more than just a fling.

Judi could hardly wait to get home to check her e-mail. She knew better than to use her company computer for personal use. She booted up the machine before she even changed clothes, but there was no message from Harry. She wrote a short note and hit the enter key, hoping she'd have a reply before dinner. But she received no reply. Nor did she get one the following night, or the night after that.

A fling.

That was all they'd shared, after all.

On the following Monday, Pam called to ask Judi out for lunch. "But we already had our once-a-year lunch," Judi protested.

"You're my sister. Isn't that enough of a reason to get together to talk?"

"I suppose. But we have to meet near my office. I'm out of vacation time until June when it starts accruing once again."

"Name the place, and I'll be there at noon."

Judi picked a diner around the corner from her office.

Pam was already waiting when Judi arrived at 12:05. "Sorry I'm late," she said and shrugged out of her coat. She picked up the menu, turning to the section marked sandwiches. "So, what's new?"

"With me? Not a thing. Our trip to the mountains was a disaster. The boys caught the flu, and our room smelled like urine. They came in and cleaned the rug, but it still smelled the entire time we were there."

"I'm sorry you had such a bad time," Judi said and gave a sigh of relief that she hadn't allowed Pam to talk her into going on the trip with them.

"Aren't you going to tell me more about your holiday?" She said the last word as though it was an insult.

"The English call their vacations holiday."

"So this Harry guy is English?"

"Was. He's got dual citizenship."

"So, he's not loyal to either country," Pam accused.

"More like he's loyal to both."

"Have you heard from him since you got home?"

Judi lowered her gaze to the menu. "Once or twice via e-mail." The truth was, she hadn't heard from him at all, which was heartbreaking, but not entirely unexpected.

"Brad did some poking around."

"What do you mean?"

"When you told me this guy had asked you to marry him, I had Brad do a background check on the guy."

"Oh, Pam—please tell me you're joking."

"I'm not.

"Would you like to know just what kind of a creep this guy is?"

"I don't suppose I have much choice," Judi said, setting the menu aside. She'd lost her appetite.

"Harry Powell; address four five six seven Calle Blanco."

That was Harry's address all right.

"Married to Doris, with three children between the ages of five and twelve; William, Nicholas, and Olivia."

"That can't be. I've been to his house. It's a small bungalow—no room for a family."

"Of course not, they live in England."

Judi felt her cheeks grow hot.

Pam looked back down to the paper before her. "He told you he was an accountant, right?"

"Yes," Judi answered warily.

"Well, he's not. He's actually a tour guide. He doesn't own that house, he rents it. And he's broke."

"Why are you telling me all this?" Judi demanded.

"Because I don't want you making a mistake that will ruin your life. I still can't believe how foolish you've behaved."

Judi said nothing, fighting tears.

"I hope you're not going to stay in contact with that gigolo now that you know the truth."

"You've certainly given me a lot to think about," and part of it was anger at how cruel Pam had been to share this information with her.

"Do yourself a favor; forget the guy," Pam advised. "You'll only get your heart broken."

Too late for that, Judi admitted to herself. She'd fallen for Harry hook, line, and sinker. And she did feel foolish. Who else would Pam share this information with? Bill, so he could condemn her, too, plus all Pam's friends, their cousins, and no doubt anyone else who would listen.

Judi shrugged back into the sleeves of her coat. "I've got to go."

"But you haven't eaten lunch yet."

"I don't want any lunch."

"I'm sorry I had to be the one to tell you all this, but you needed to know. You're just too trusting, Judi. You always have been."

Judi stood. "I'll talk to you later," she said but had no intention of speaking to Pam any time soon.

Weeks went by and Judi heard nothing from Harry. Not an e-mail, not a phone call, not a card. Pam was right. He'd taken advantage of her. Not that he'd asked her for money, or to even pay for the dinners and lunches they'd shared. And he hadn't pressured her into having sex with him, either. She had enjoyed every minute she'd spent with Harry, and she'd fallen for him. She'd been incredibly foolish to expect they would stay in contact once she left the island, but it was a lesson learned. And eventually, she'd be able to think of Harry a bit more charitably than she did just then.

January rolled over to February. With each passing day, Judi thought less and less about Harry. It started to seem as though the week she'd spent in Puerto Rico was all a dream. A pleasant dream, but a dream nonetheless. Ted noticed that she'd taken on more work, and rewarded her with a modest and long overdue raise. She'd bank the extra cash to save for a home of her own. She wanted to change her life, make it very different from what it had been before her Christmastime holiday.

It was on a Thursday that she noticed squeals of delight coming from a number of other cubicles around her. She got up to raid the break room's coffee pot and noticed that several of the other women in the office had vases of flowers on their desks. It was then she realized it was Valentine's Day. Would this be the day she heard from Harry?

Judi found it hard to concentrate that day, waiting for a phone call from the building's reception desk telling her to come and retrieve her own vase of flowers. But the call never came.

Judi went home to warm a frozen dinner, watch a little TV, and go to bed early.

The summer came and went, as did the fall. Carol invited her for Thanksgiving, but she'd declined, preferring to roast a chicken at home, and spending the day alone. Then suddenly Christmastime was upon her again. Pam and her family made different holiday plans, deciding to head to Disney World, even though her kids were probably far too old for it. Pam intended to bake in the sun the entire week. Bill and his family were having Christmas dinner with Jean's family. Neither of them invited Judi to join them, and they didn't even arrange a lunch together before the big day. That was all right with Judi, who was still put out that they'd accepted her gifts but hadn't reciprocated with even a Christmas card.

The Secret Santa went on as usual, and this time several people brought bottles of wine. Judi's prize was an amaryllis bulb. All she needed to do was water it and she'd be reminded of the island paradise she'd visited the year before.

But she didn't want to remember. She wanted to forget it.

Still, on the day before Christmas Eve, she found herself packing a bag and heading for the airport. Seats were hard to come by on short notice and she flew standby to Florida, and again to Puerto Rico. She arrived after dark, hailed a cab, and had it take her to a much more modest hotel than she'd stayed in the year before.

Christmas Eve morning, she headed for the beach. Was she looking for Harry? She knew where he lived. If she was that determined to find him, she could go straight there and wait for him to show.

As she sat on the beach, she found that rather than relax, she grew angrier with every minute that passed.

She spent the day slathering her body with sunscreen and scanning the faces of every man who walked by.

The sun was beginning to set when she called it a day. She'd never turned on her e-reader, and she hadn't spoken a word to any of her fellow vacationers, but somehow she didn't feel lonely. She was too angry for that.

And yet, why was she angry?

Because Harry had asked her to marry him. Because he hadn't told her about the family in England he'd left behind. Because he wasn't an accountant like he'd said.

Fury rose within her. She stalked back to the hotel, changed clothes, and hailed a cab. She wasn't going to wait another second for him to find her; she was determined to track him down.

Calle Blanco looked exactly the same as it had the year before when Harry had invited her to his house and cooked her a delicious meal. She got out of the cab, giving the driver a good tip. "You want me to wait?" he asked.

She shook her head. As it was, she'd have to raid her new house fund to pay for this last-minute trip. She watched as the cab took off, and then marched up to Harry's door, rapping so hard on it that her knuckles hurt.

The door opened and a young black woman dressed in white stood behind her. "Can I help you?" she asked.

"I'm looking for Harry Powell."

"Are you a friend of his?"

"Yes. At least I thought so."

"Then please, come in. I'm sure he'd love to see an old friend."

"Not so old," Judi said. "We only met a year ago."

"Judi?" the woman guessed. "Are you Harry's Judi?"

"I don't know. Does he know more than one?"

The woman ushered Judi in. "Follow me out to the courtyard."

Judi did so, feeling her anger grow with each step. For days she'd been rehearsing what she'd say when she finally stood face to face with him.

"Harry, it's Judi. She's come to visit you," the woman called.

She stepped aside and Judi was taken aback at the sight of the wheelchair.

"Harry?" Judi called.

"He's probably asleep. He likes to come outside in the evenings, but usually dozes."

"Are you his caregiver?" Judi asked and suddenly realized why the woman was dressed all in white.

The woman nodded. "I'm LaToya. I've been taking care of him for the last two months. He's doing well with the crutches, but at the end of the day it's just easier for him to be wheeled outside."

"What happened?"

"A car accident—a year ago next week. A drunk driver at ten o'clock in the morning. Can you imagine that?"

Ten o'clock. Had the accident occurred the same day—the very hour—that Harry had dropped her off at the airport? Was that why he had never contacted her?

"Where's his family. Why aren't they taking care of him?"

"Family? Harry has no family."

"I understood he had a wife and children in England."

"They are dead—for at least five years. That is why Harry came to Puerto Rico. He wanted to live in a place that had no memories of his lost family."

"Sounds like he's told you a lot about himself," Judi said.

"We have spent many hours together. I will get him ready for bed and then go home to spend Christmas with my husband and children."

Judi fought tears. This was not the reunion she had anticipated. Had Pam known the truth? Had she known that Harry had been terribly injured in an accident and kept that information from her knowing she might jump on a plane to help take care of him? The object of her anger turned from Harry to Pam. How could her own sister have been so heartless? Did she lie about everything else, too?"

"How has Harry paid for his care?"

"He has lived modestly since he came to Puerto Rico, but now his savings are nearly depleted. He hasn't been able to work, but hopes to start in the next month or so. His recovery has been slow, but remarkable. At first, no one thought he would ever speak again, but he surprised them. They said he would never walk, but he can, with crutches."

"Why didn't he contact me?" she asked, her voice cracking with emotion.

"Because he knew you would come. He did not want you to see him the way he is."

Harry's head bobbed up; he must have awakened from his nap. "LaToya," he called. "Is it time for bed?"

LaToya stepped in front of the wheelchair. "I have a Christmas surprise for you."

"Surprise?" Harry repeated.

LaToya gestured for Judi to step forward. She hesitated, afraid to see his face, afraid that he might not remember her, afraid that she might not be able to handle seeing him hurt.

"Come, come," LaToya encouraged, and somehow Judi found the strength to step forward.

"Harry?" she called.

Harry's head jerked up. "Judi?" he called, his voice sounding hoarse.

LaToya stepped aside and Judi took her place, crouching down in front of the wheelchair. She bit her lip at the sight of the scar that ran along the left side of his face. "I'm here," she said and reached for his hand.

"Tell me this isn't a dream. Tell me this is real."

"It's real. I'm here," Judi said as a tear cascaded down her cheek.

Harry reached out and brushed it aside. "You came back to me."

"Yes, I did. I'm only sorry I didn't come sooner. I would have, if I'd have known."

Harry's eyes filled with tears. "I knew you would. But I wouldn't let them contact you. You don't deserve to be saddled with a cripple."

"LaToya tells me you've made a fantastic recovery, and that you'll soon be back to your old self."

"I didn't think it would be possible. Miracles don't happen to people like me. But you're here, and that can only be a miracle."

"It's not a miracle. It was love that brought me. I love you, Harry. I've missed you. And I won't leave you."

He shook his head. "No, you have a life back in Cleveland. I wouldn't wish myself upon you. You took care of your parents for so long. I won't allow you to do the same for me."

"We don't have to talk about any of that right now. Can't we just enjoy being together right now, right on Christmas Eve?"

"Is it Christmas again?" Harry asked. Judi nodded. "Then you are the best present I could have received."

Judi fumbled for the chain around her neck, pulling it out from her blouse and showing him the sea glass. "I've worn it every day since we parted. I'll never take it off."

Harry smiled. "Merry Christmas, my love."

Judi leaned in to kiss him. They kissed again and again.

ALSO BY LORRAINE BARTLETT

THE VICTORIA SQUARE MYSTERIES

A Crafty Killing

The Walled Flower

One Hot Murder

Dead, Bath and Beyond (with Laurie Cass)

Yule Be Dead (with Gayle Leeson)

Murder, Ink (with Gayle Leeson)

Recipes To Die For: A Victoria Square Cookbook

Check my website for e-book editions for the UK, EI, AU and NZ.

LIFE ON VICTORIA SQUARE (*A companion series to the Victoria Square Mysteries*)

Carving Out A Path

A Basket Full of Bargains

The Broken Teacup

It's Tutu Much

The Reluctant Bride

THE LOTUS BAY MYSTERIES

Panty Raid (A Tori Cannon-Kathy Grant mini mystery)

With Baited Breath

Christmas At Swans Nest

A Reel Catch

BLYTHE COVE MANOR

A Dream Weekend

A Final Gift

An Unexpected Visitor

Grape Expectations

TALES OF TELENIA (adventure-fantasy)

THRESHOLD

JOURNEY

TREACHERY

SHORT STORIES

Love & Murder: A Bargain-Priced Collection of Short Stories

Happy Holidays? (A Collection of Christmas Stories)

An Unconditional Love

Love Heals

Blue Christmas

Prisoner of Love

We're So Sorry, Uncle Albert

Writing as L.L. Bartlett

The Jeff Resnick Mysteries

Murder On The Mind

Dead In Red

Room At The Inn

Cheated By Death

Bound By Suggestion

Dark Waters

Shattered Spirits

Jeff Resnick's Personal Files

Evolution: Jeff Resnick's Backstory

A Jeff Resnick Six Pack

When The Spirit Moves You

Bah! Humbug

Cold Case

Spooked!

Crybaby

Eyewitness

A Part of the Pattern

Other Stories

Abused: A Daughter's Story

Off Script

Writing as Lorna Barrett

THE BOOKTOWN MYSTERIES

Murder Is Binding

Bookmarked For Death

Bookplate Special

Chapter & Hearse

Sentenced To Death

Murder On The Half Shelf

Not The Killing Type

Book Clubbed

A Fatal Chapter

Title Wave

A Just Clause

Poisoned Pages

A Killer Edition

WITH THE COZY CHICKS

The Cozy Chicks Kitchen

Tea Time With The Cozy Chicks

www.ingramcontent.com/pod-product-compliance
Lightning Source LLC
Chambersburg PA
CBHW071829190726
48292CB00005B/1679